THE FLYING BEAVER BROTHERS
AND THE MUD-SLINGING MOLES

MAXWELL EATON III

ALFRED A. KNOPF
NEW YORK

FOR KEE

THIS IS A BORZOI BOOK PUBLISHED BY ALFRED A. KNOPF

This is a work of fiction. Names, characters, places, and incidents either are the product of the author's imagination or are used fictitiously. Any resemblance to actual persons, living or dead, events, or locales is entirely coincidental.

Visit us on the Web! randomhouse.com/kids

Educators and librarians, for a variety of teaching tools, visit us at RHTeachersLibrarians.com

Library of Congress Cataloging-in-Publication Data
Eaton, Maxwell.
The flying beaver brothers and the mud-slinging moles / Maxwell Eaton III. — 1st ed.
p. cm.
Summary: Ace and Bub stand up to nearsighted Captain Jojo and his crew of moles, who are stealing dirt from Beaver Island to make their own island home bigger.
ISBN 978-0-449-81019-4 (trade) — ISBN 978-0-449-81020-0 (lib. bdg.) —
ISBN 978-0-449-81021-7 (ebook)
1. Graphic novels. [1. Graphic novels. 2. Beavers—Fiction. 3. Moles—Fiction.
4. Islands—Fiction. 5. Conservation of natural resources—Fiction.] I. Title.
PZ7.7.E18Fmm 2013
741.5'973—dc23
2012034046

The illustrations in this book were created using pen and ink with digital coloring.

MANUFACTURED IN MALAYSIA

July 2013

10 9 8 7 6 5 4 3 2 1

First Edition

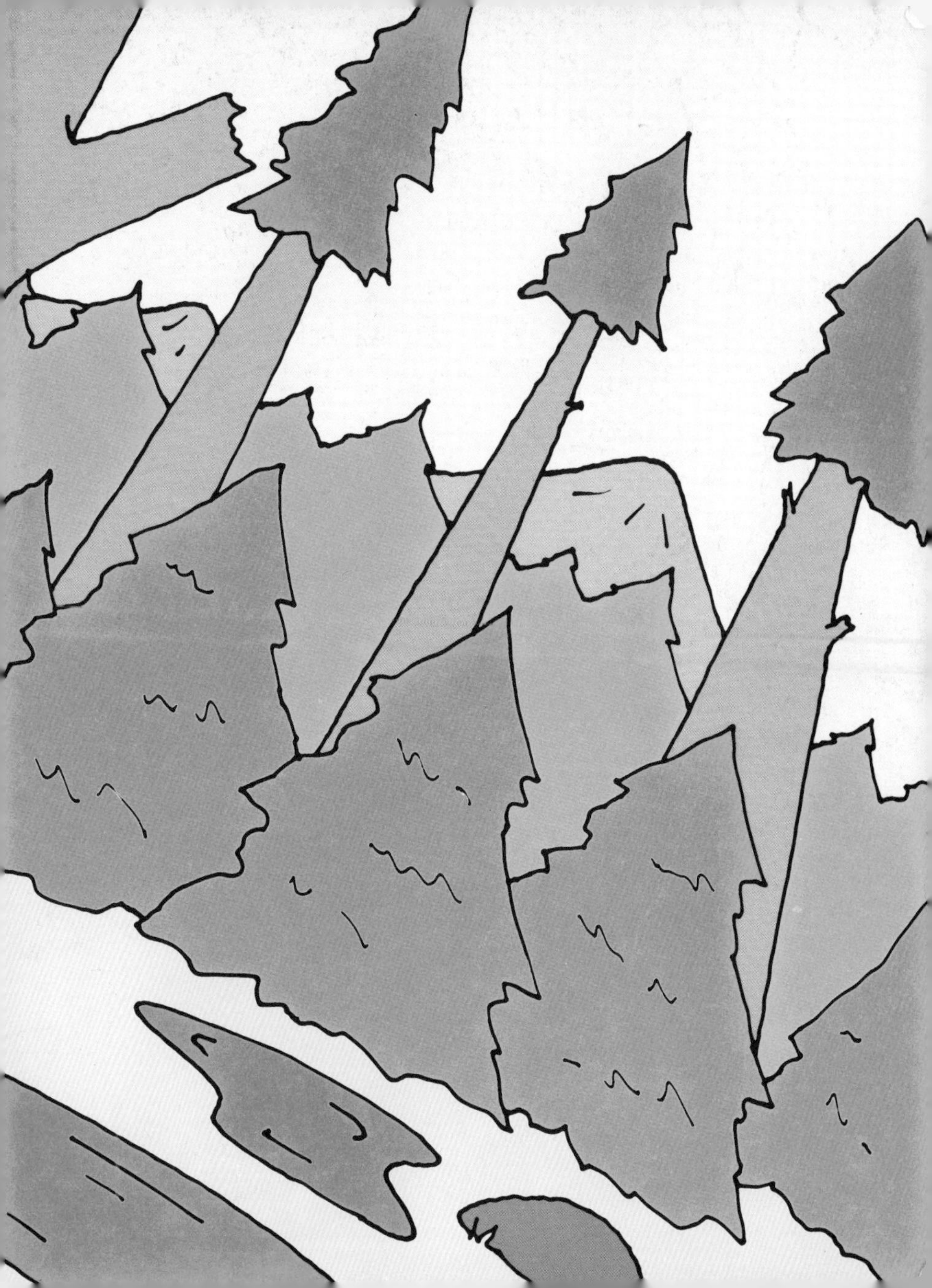

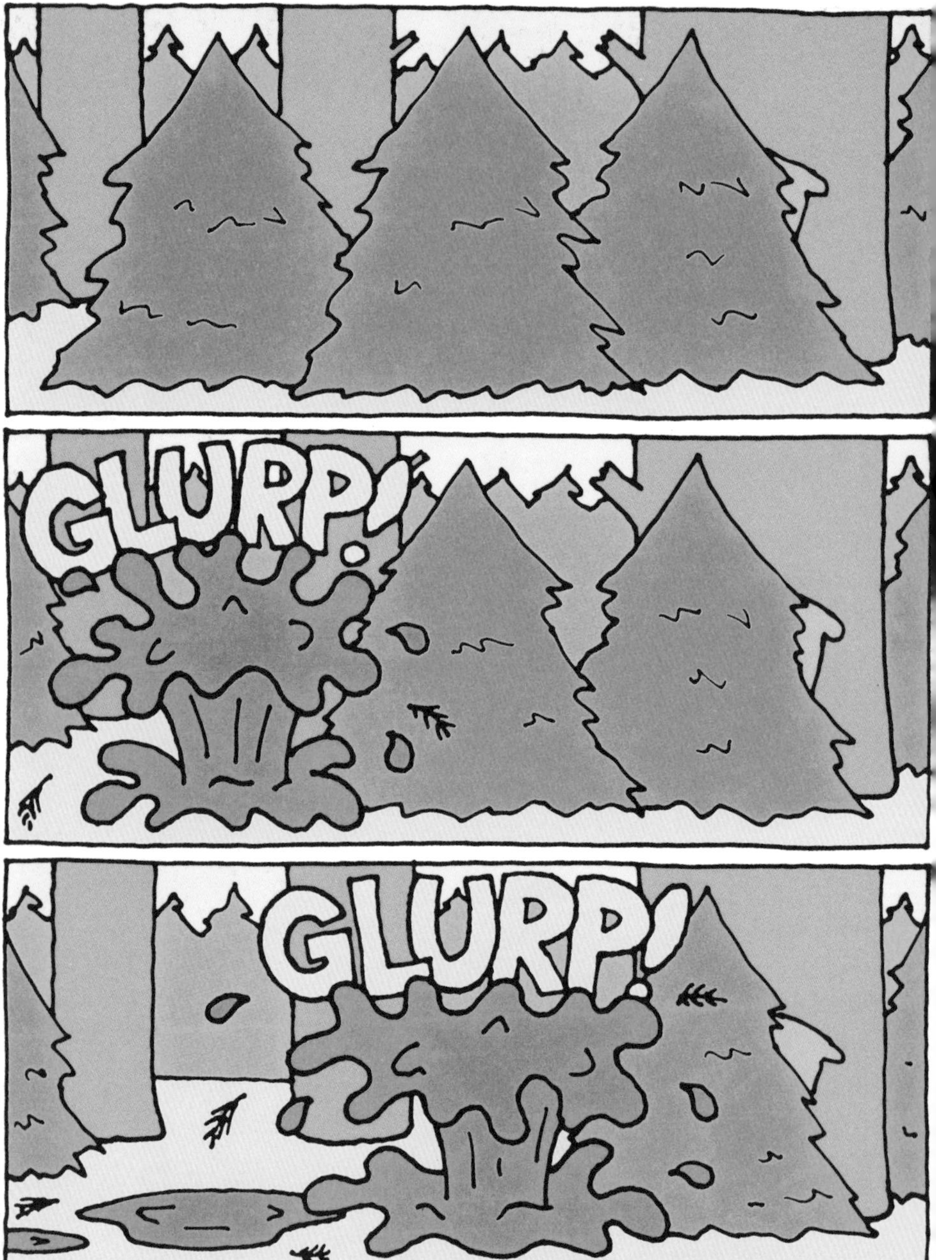
GLURP!
GLURP!

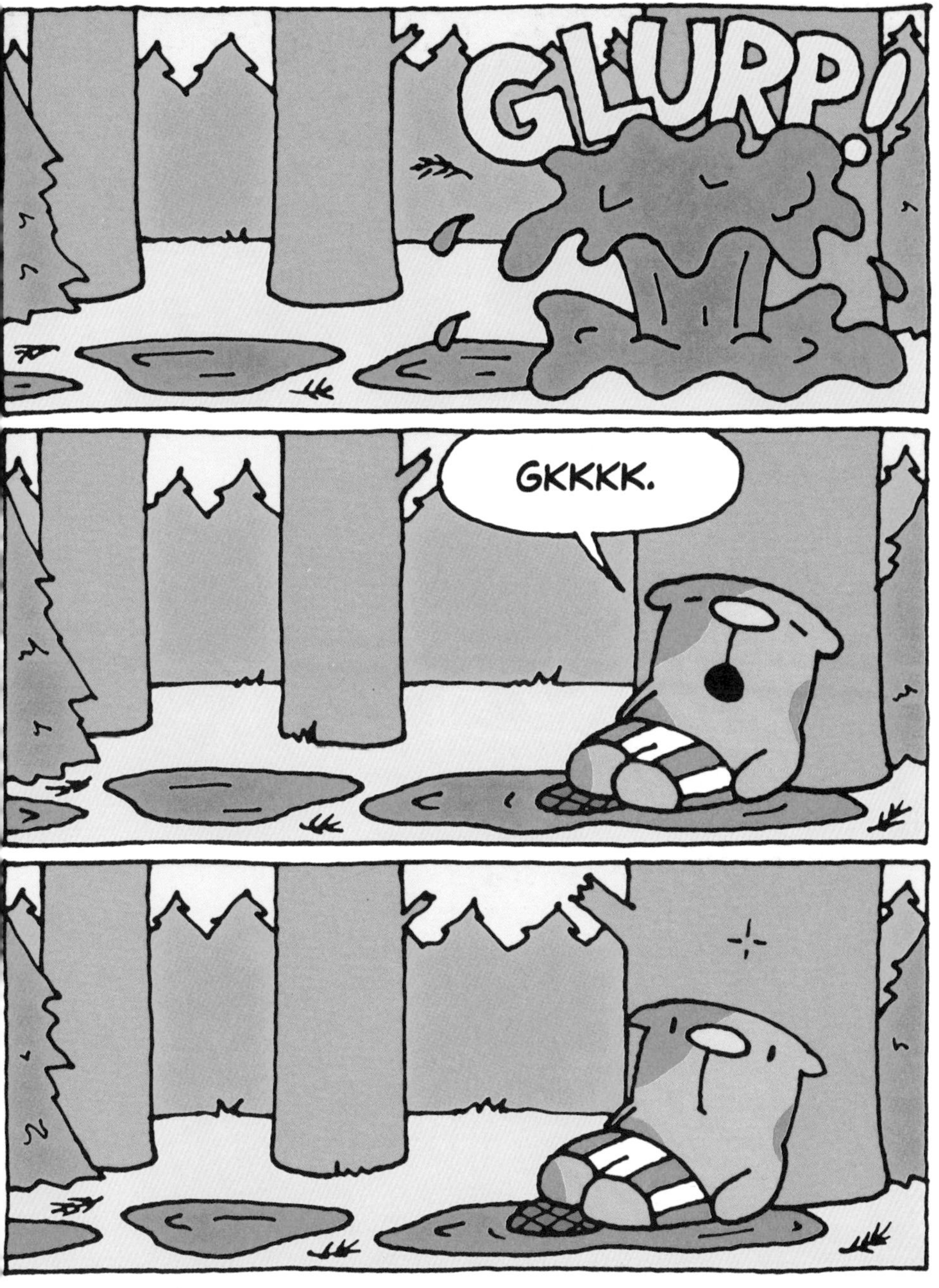
GLURP!
GKKKK.

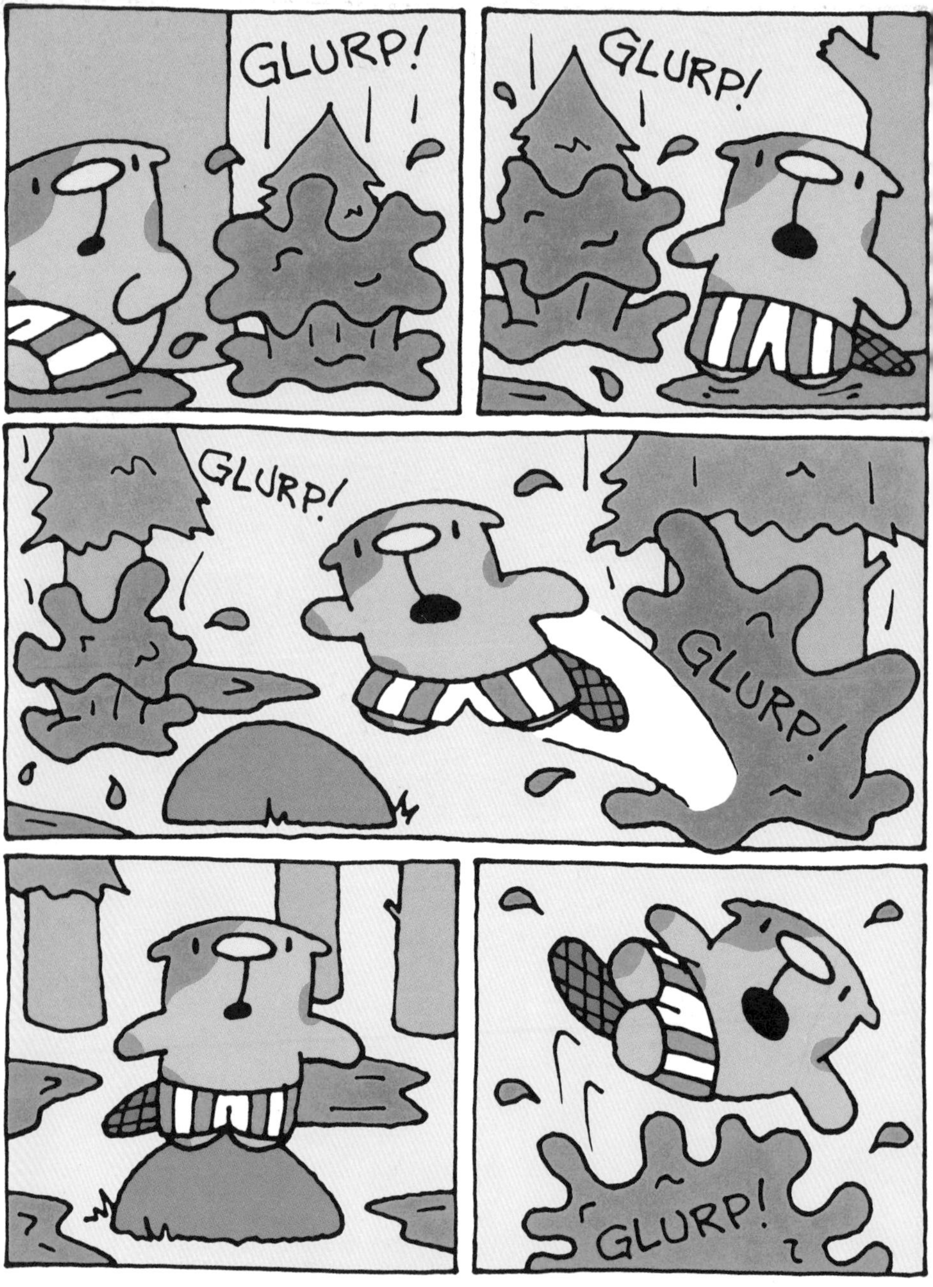
GLURP!
GLURP!
GLURP!
GLURP!
GLURP!

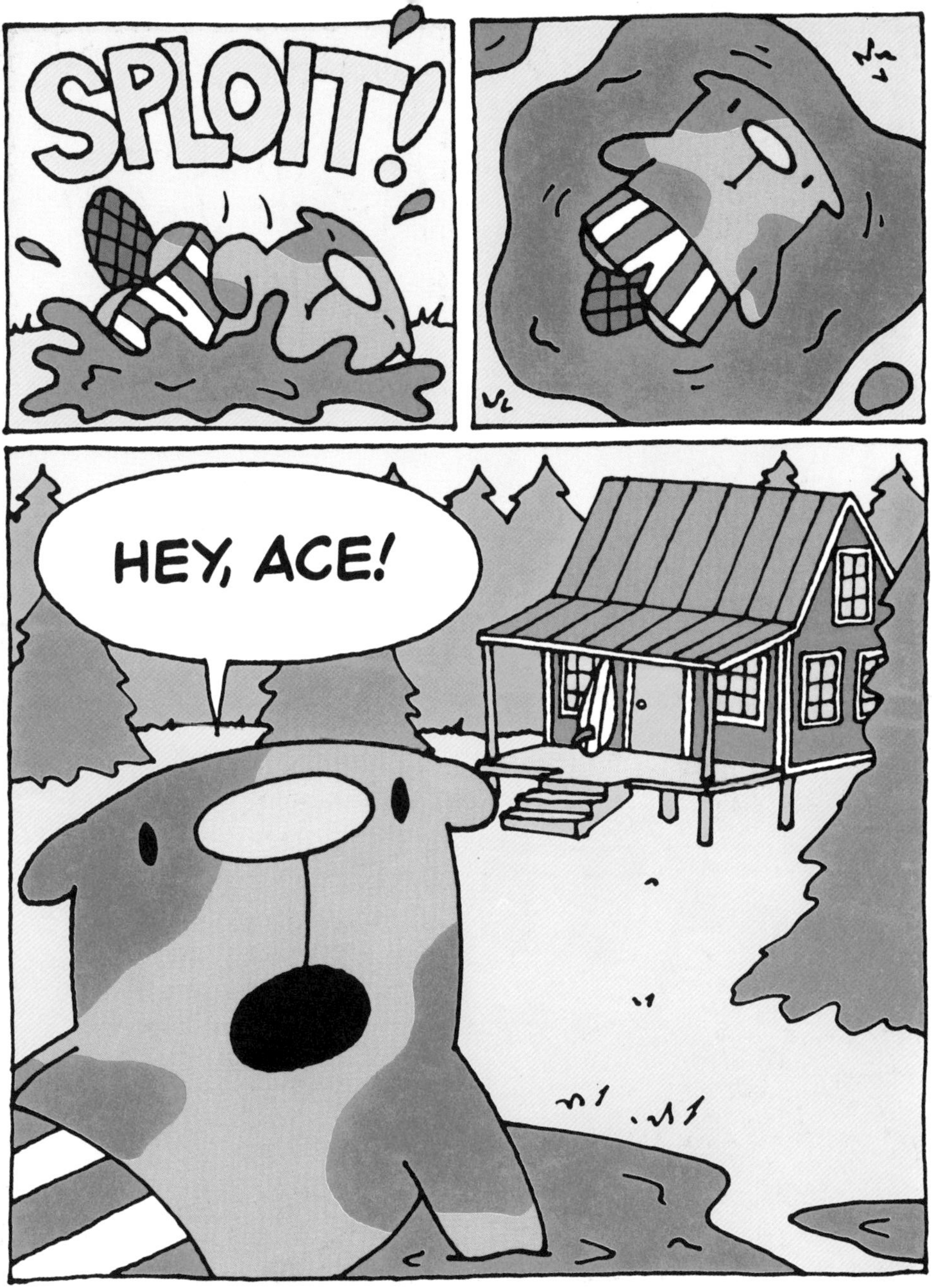
SPLOIT!
HEY, ACE!

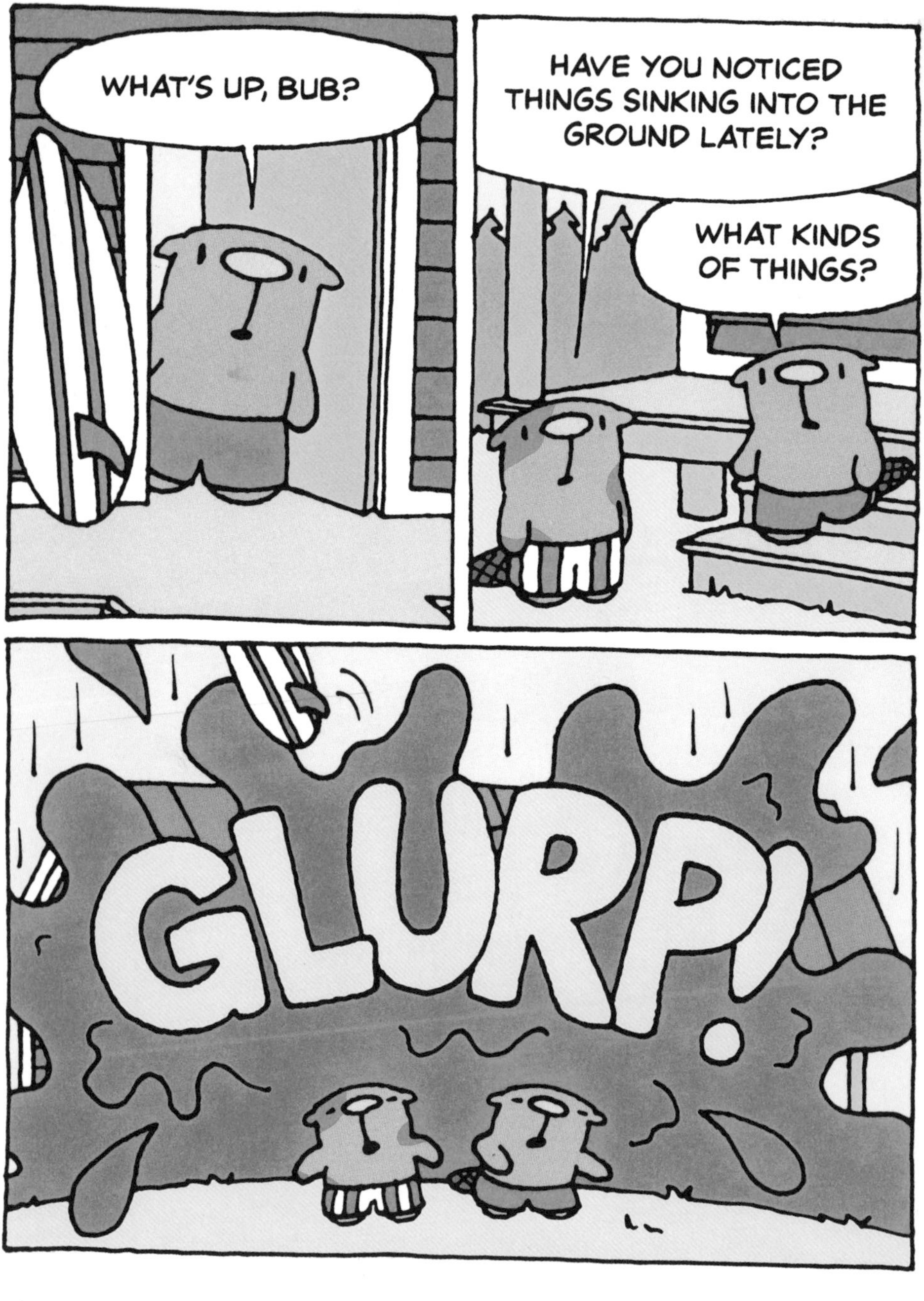
WHAT'S UP, BUB?
HAVE YOU NOTICED THINGS SINKING INTO THE GROUND LATELY?
WHAT KINDS OF THINGS?
GLURP!

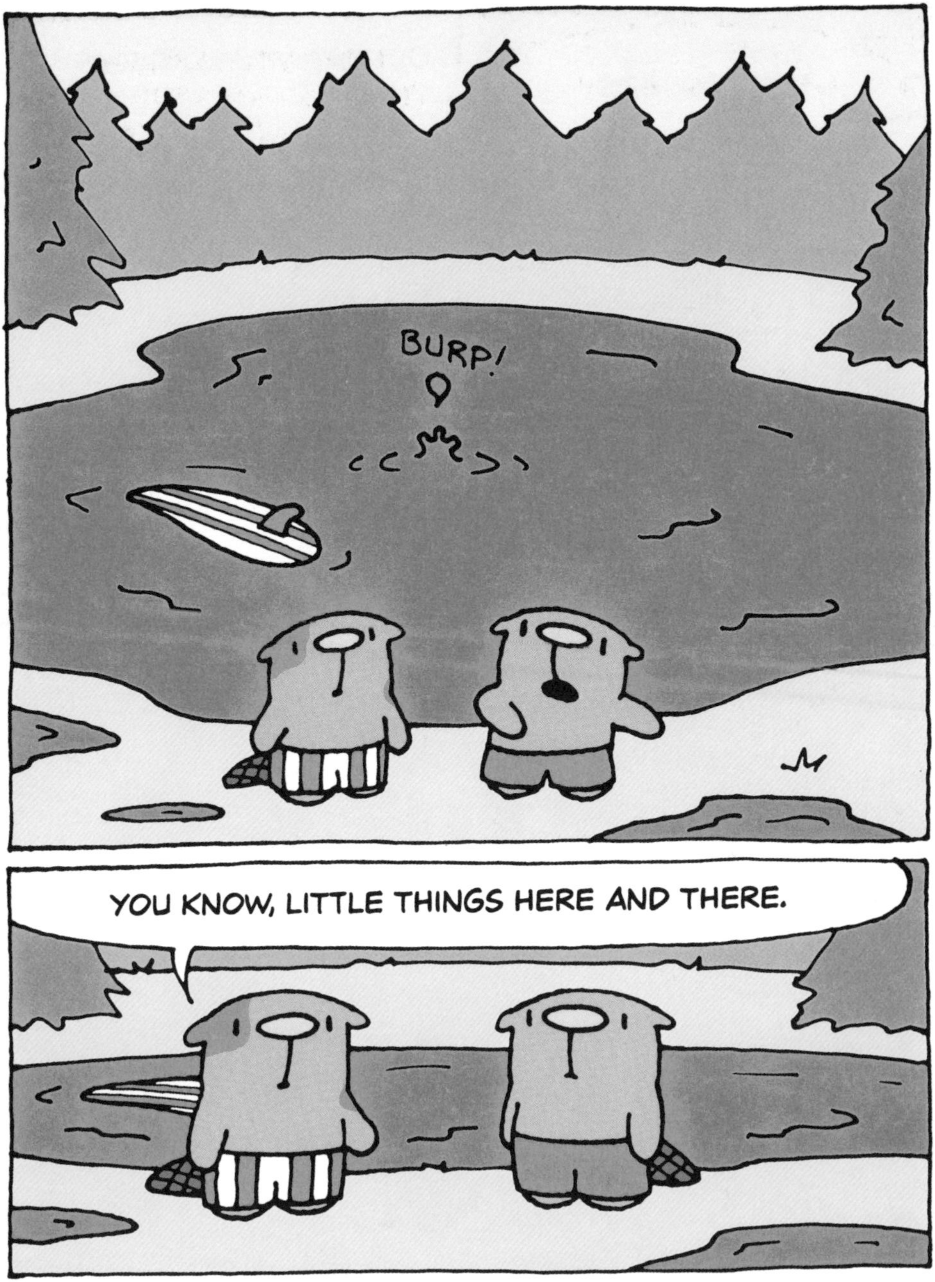
BURP!
YOU KNOW, LITTLE THINGS HERE AND THERE.

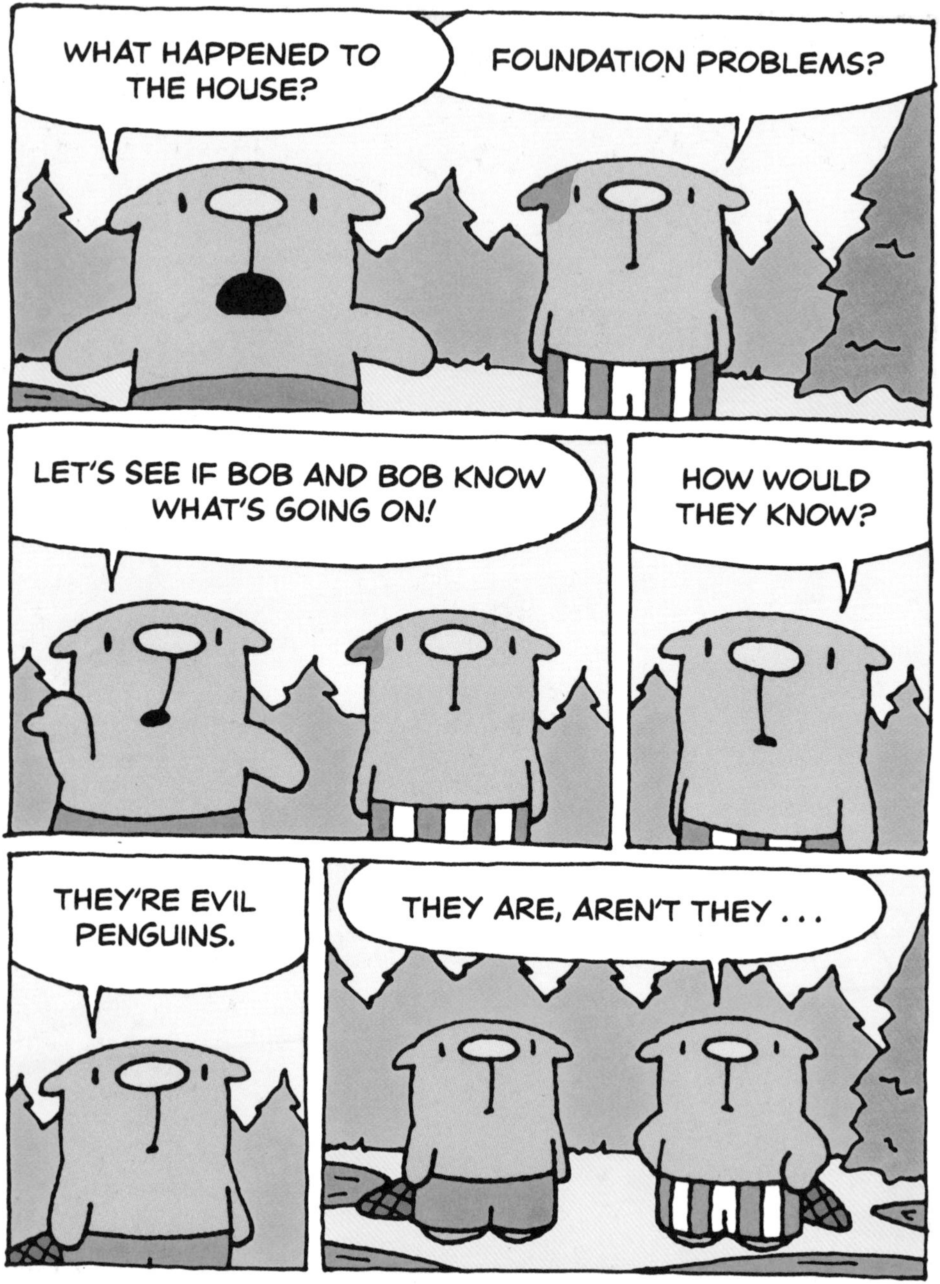
WHAT HAPPENED TO THE HOUSE?
FOUNDATION PROBLEMS?
LET'S SEE IF BOB AND BOB KNOW WHAT'S GOING ON!
HOW WOULD THEY KNOW?
THEY'RE EVIL PENGUINS.
THEY ARE, AREN'T THEY . . .

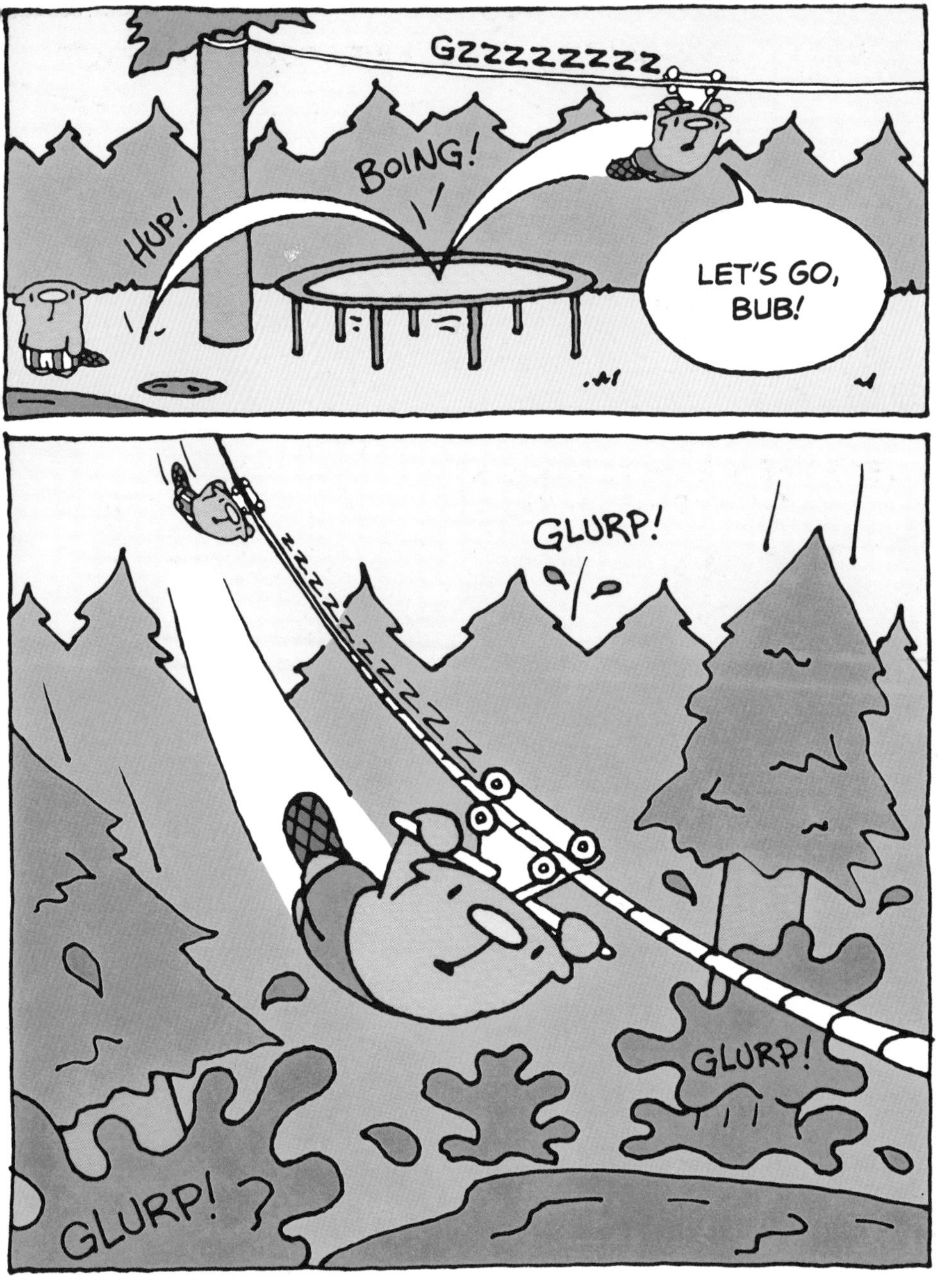
GZZZZZZZZZ
HUP!
BOING!
LET'S GO, BUB!
GLURP!
ZZZZZZZZZZ
GLURP!
GLURP!

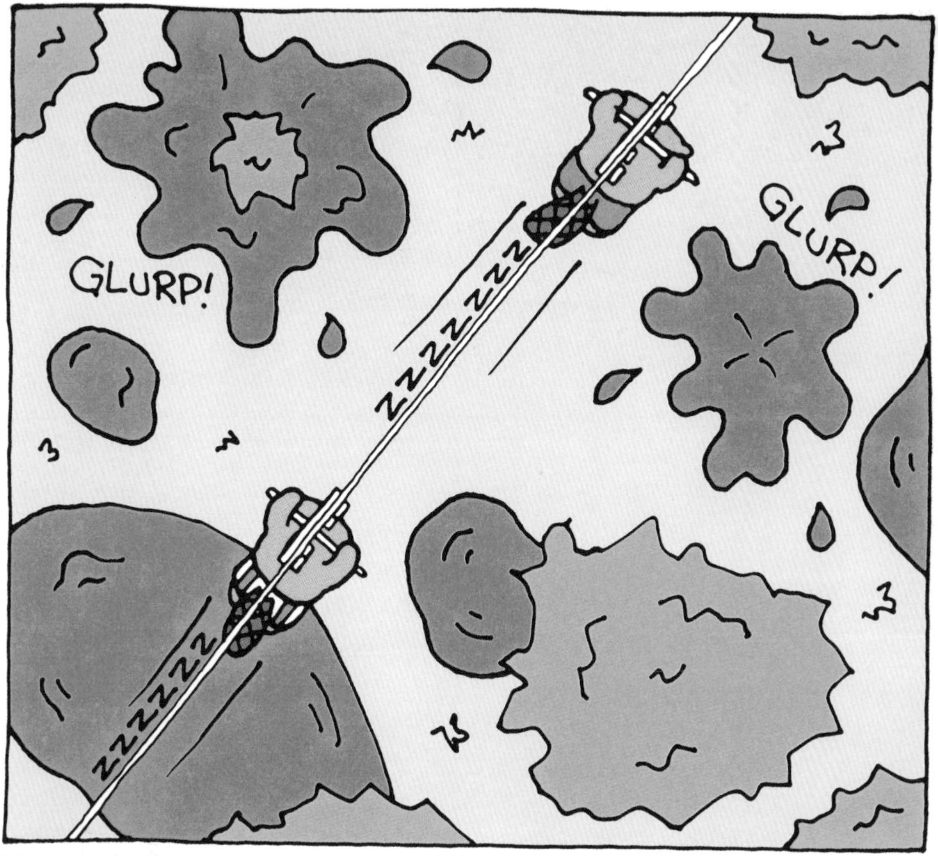
GLURP!
GLURP!
ZZZZZZZZ
ZZZZZZZ
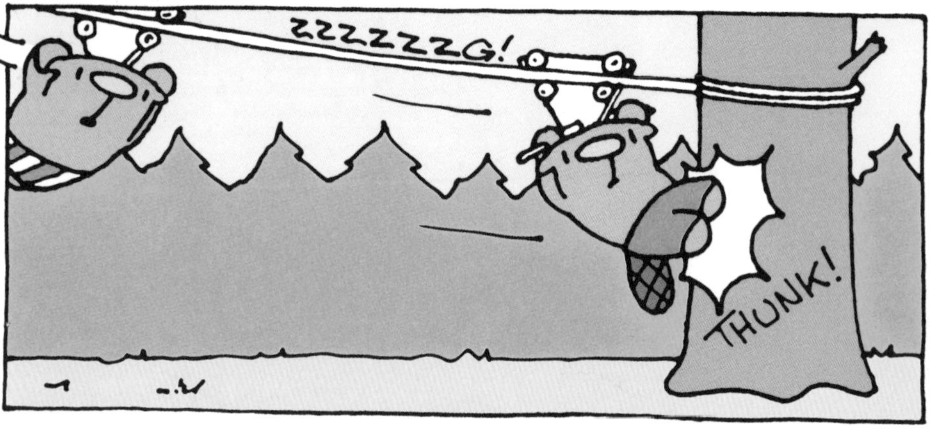
ZZZZZZZG!
THUNK!

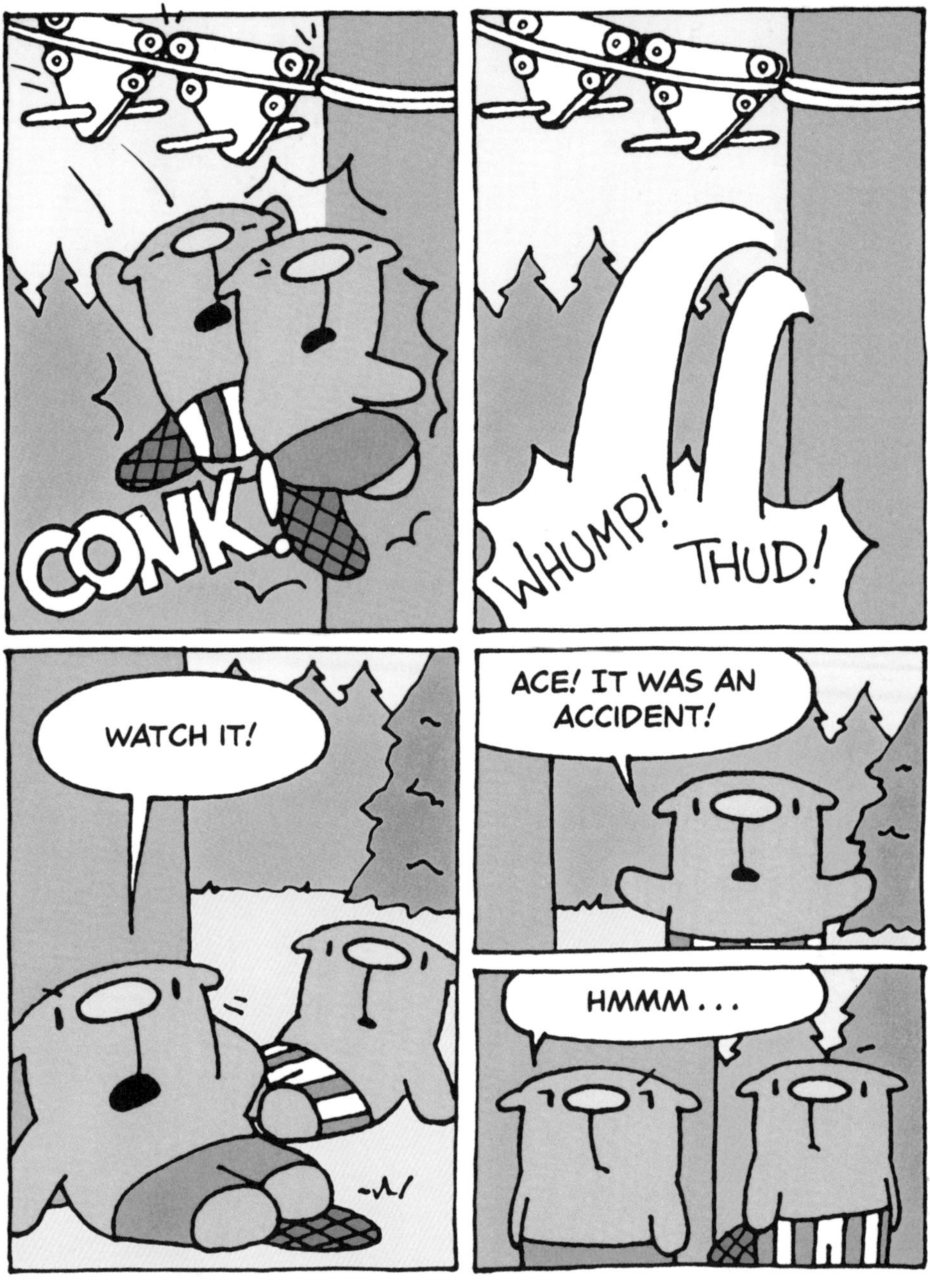
CONK!
WHUMP!
THUD!
WATCH IT!
ACE! IT WAS AN ACCIDENT!
HMMM . . .

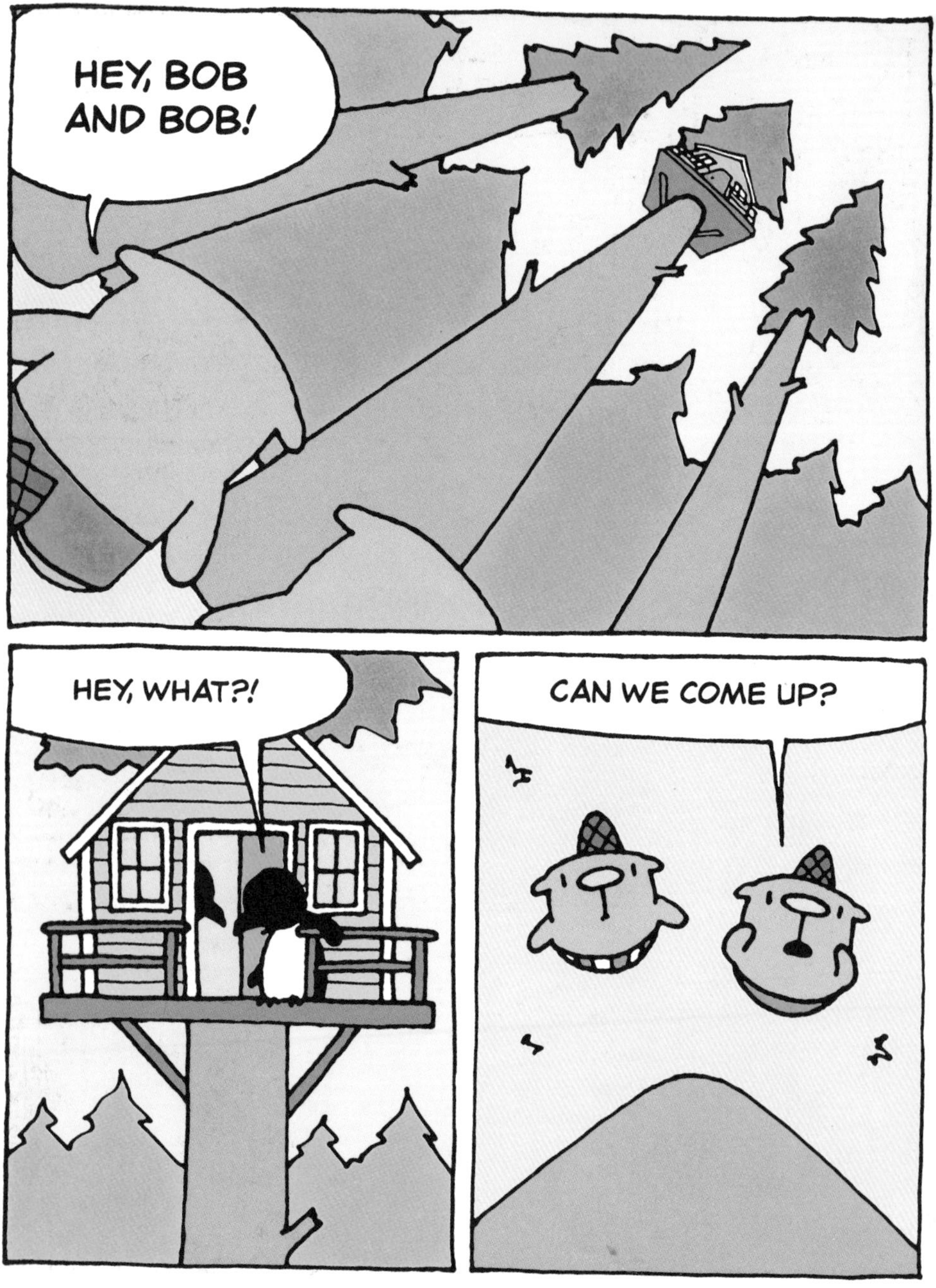
HEY, BOB
AND BOB!
HEY, WHAT?!
CAN WE COME UP?

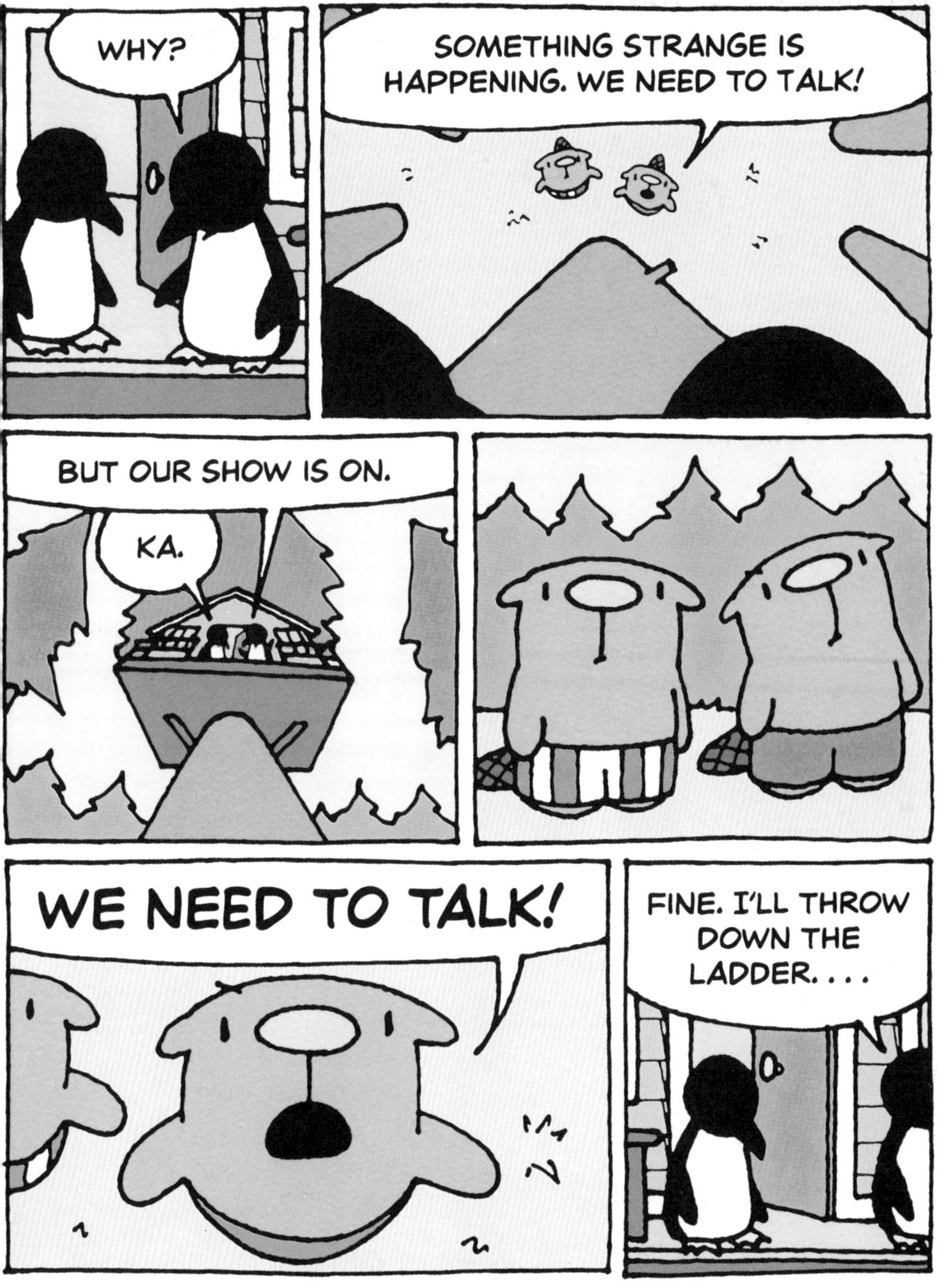
WHY?
SOMETHING STRANGE IS HAPPENING. WE NEED TO TALK!
BUT OUR SHOW IS ON.
KA.
WE NEED TO TALK!
FINE. I'LL THROW DOWN THE LADDER. . . .

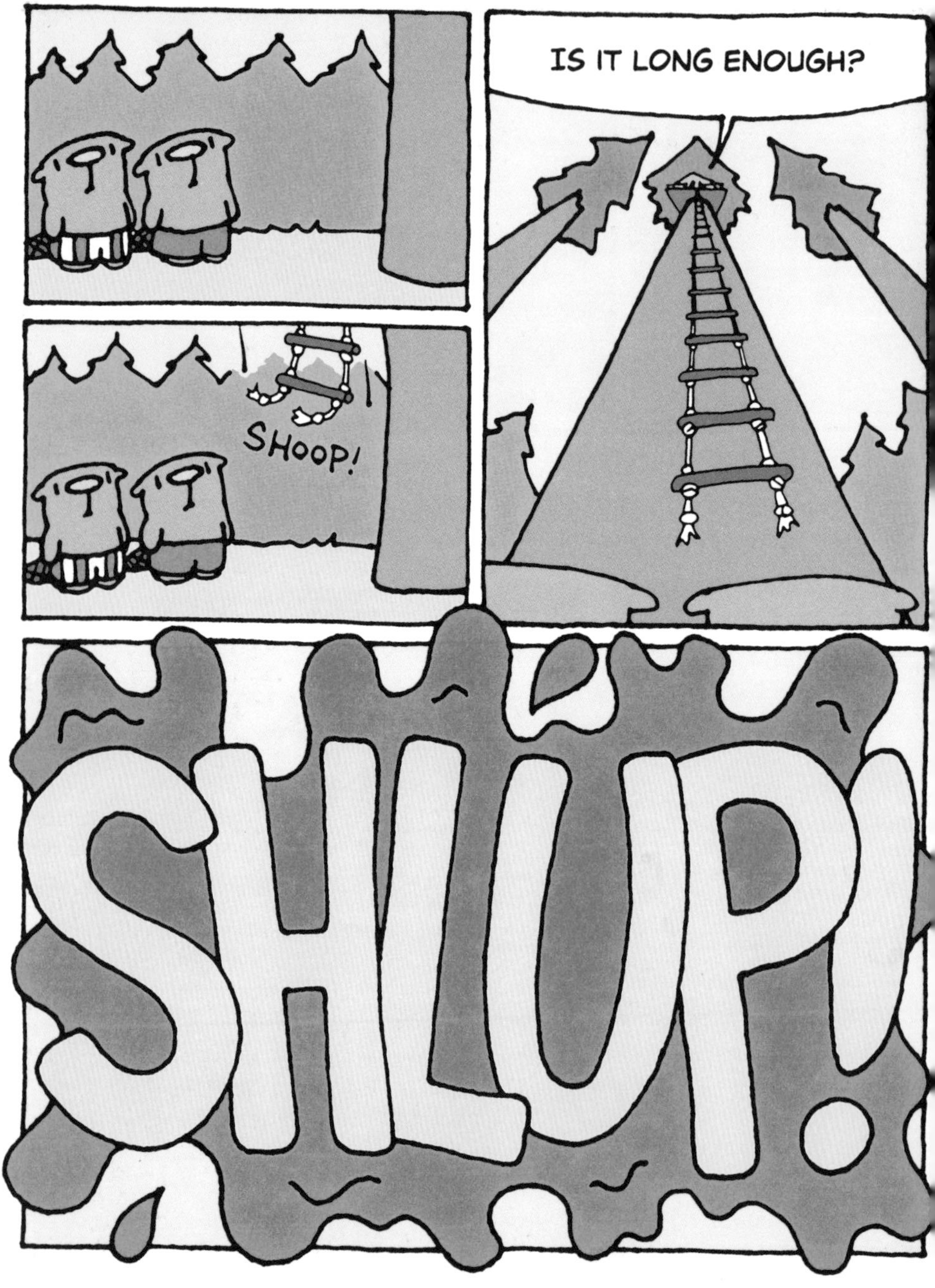
SHOOP!
IS IT LONG ENOUGH?
SHLUP!

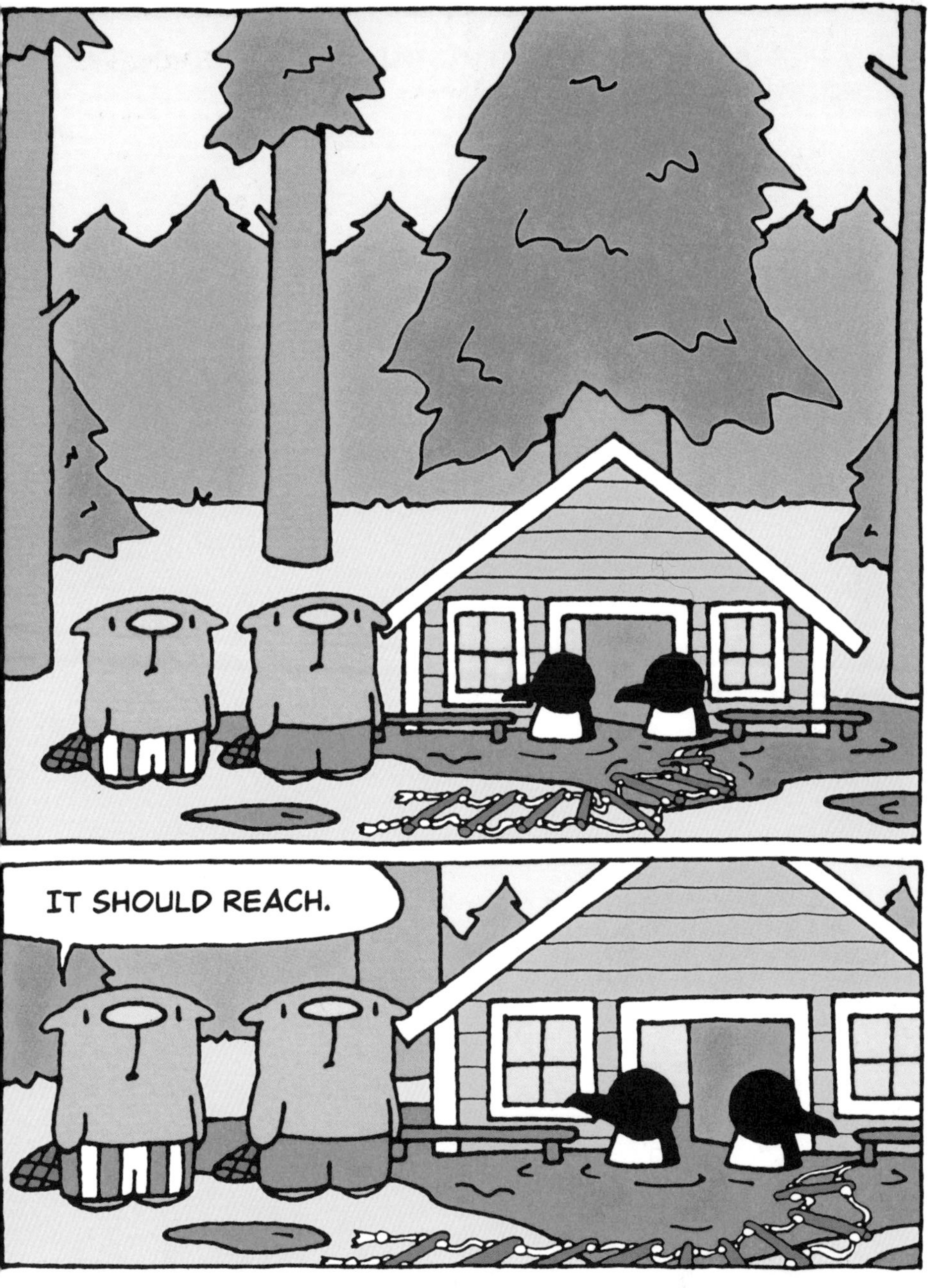
IT SHOULD REACH.

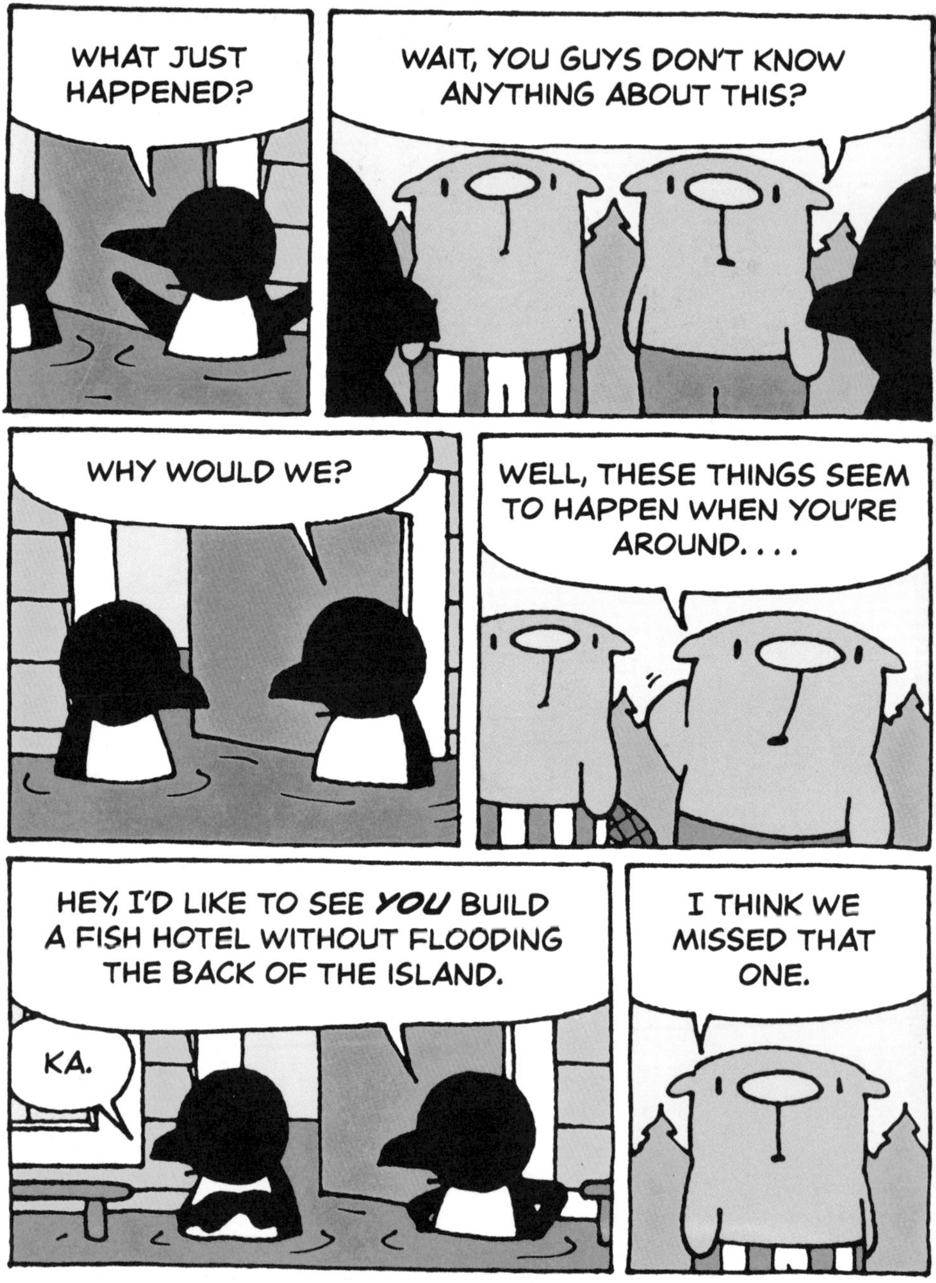
WHAT JUST HAPPENED?
WAIT, YOU GUYS DON'T KNOW ANYTHING ABOUT THIS?
WHY WOULD WE?
WELL, THESE THINGS SEEM TO HAPPEN WHEN YOU'RE AROUND. . . .
HEY, I'D LIKE TO SEE *YOU* BUILD A FISH HOTEL WITHOUT FLOODING THE BACK OF THE ISLAND.
KA.
I THINK WE MISSED THAT ONE.

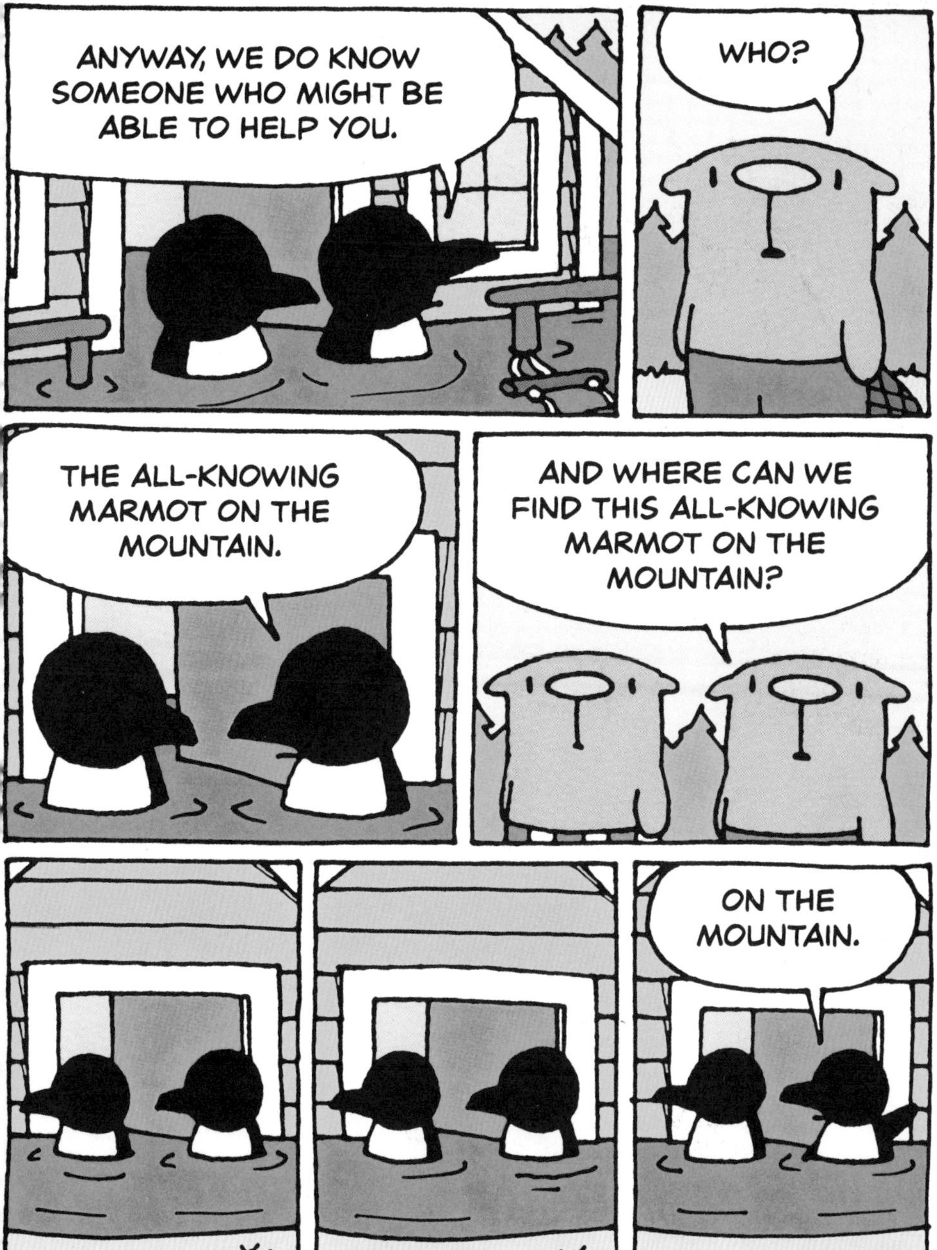
ANYWAY, WE DO KNOW SOMEONE WHO MIGHT BE ABLE TO HELP YOU.
WHO?
THE ALL-KNOWING MARMOT ON THE MOUNTAIN.
AND WHERE CAN WE FIND THIS ALL-KNOWING MARMOT ON THE MOUNTAIN?
ON THE MOUNTAIN.

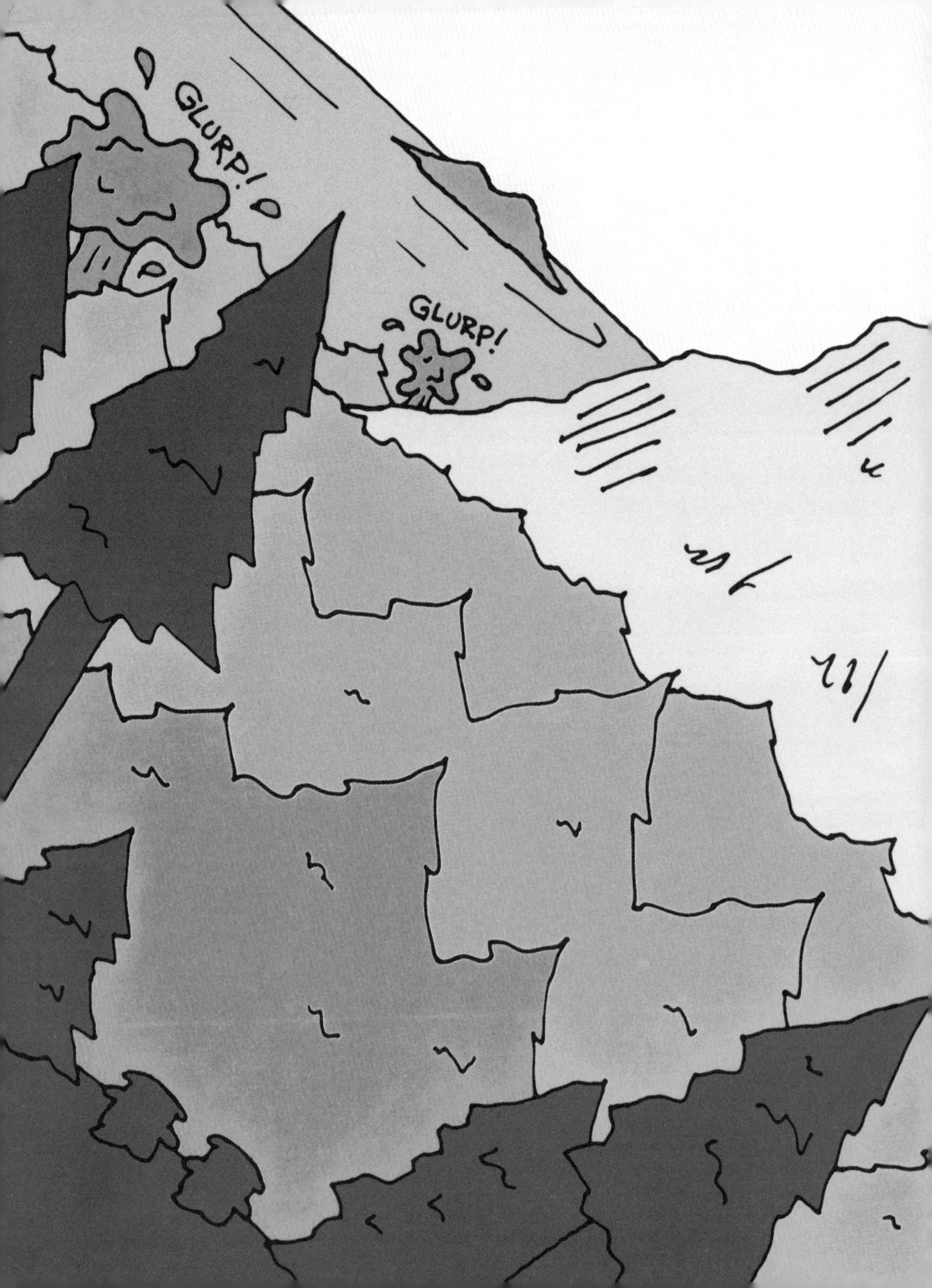
GLURP!
GLURP!

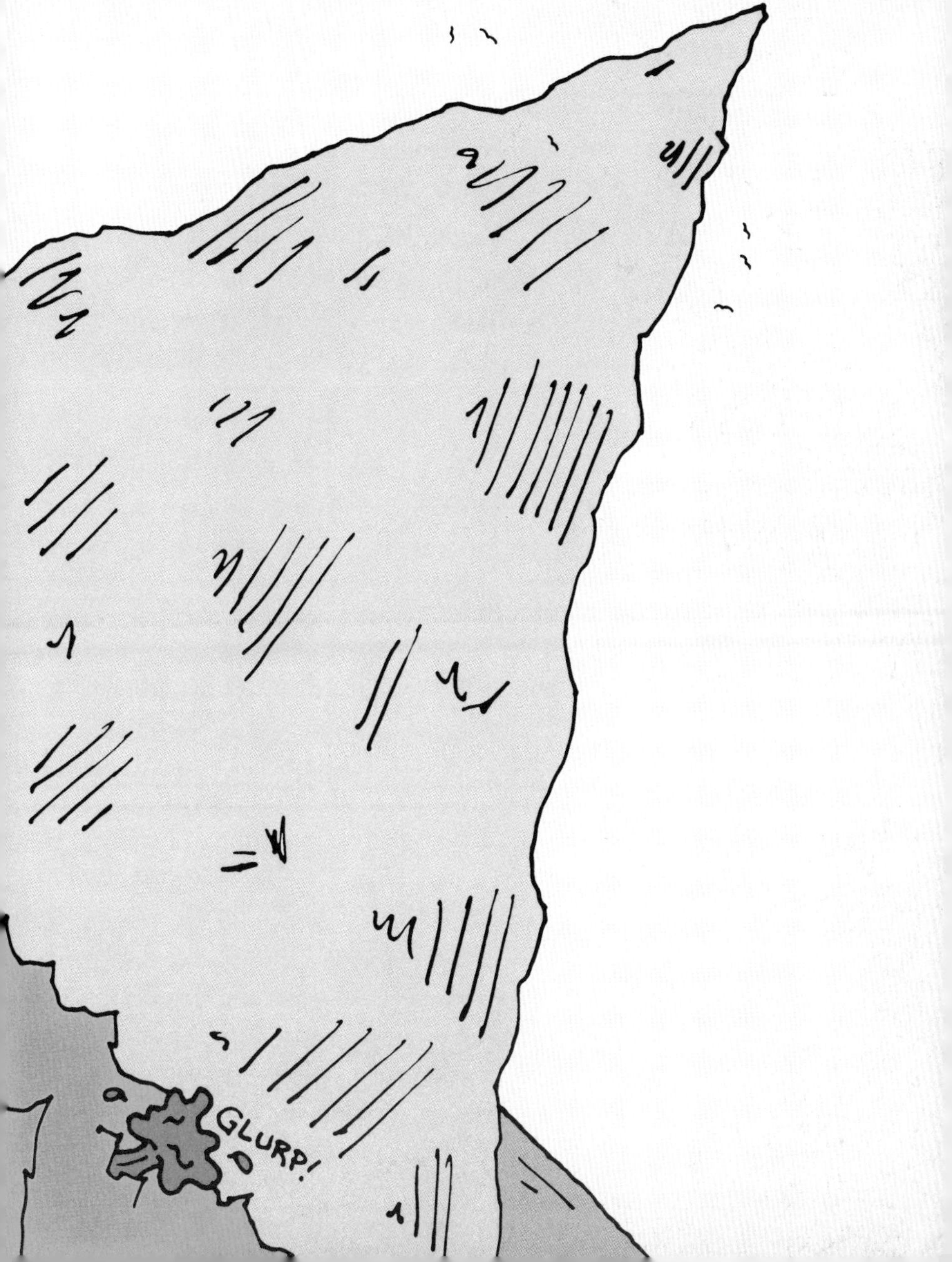
GLURP!

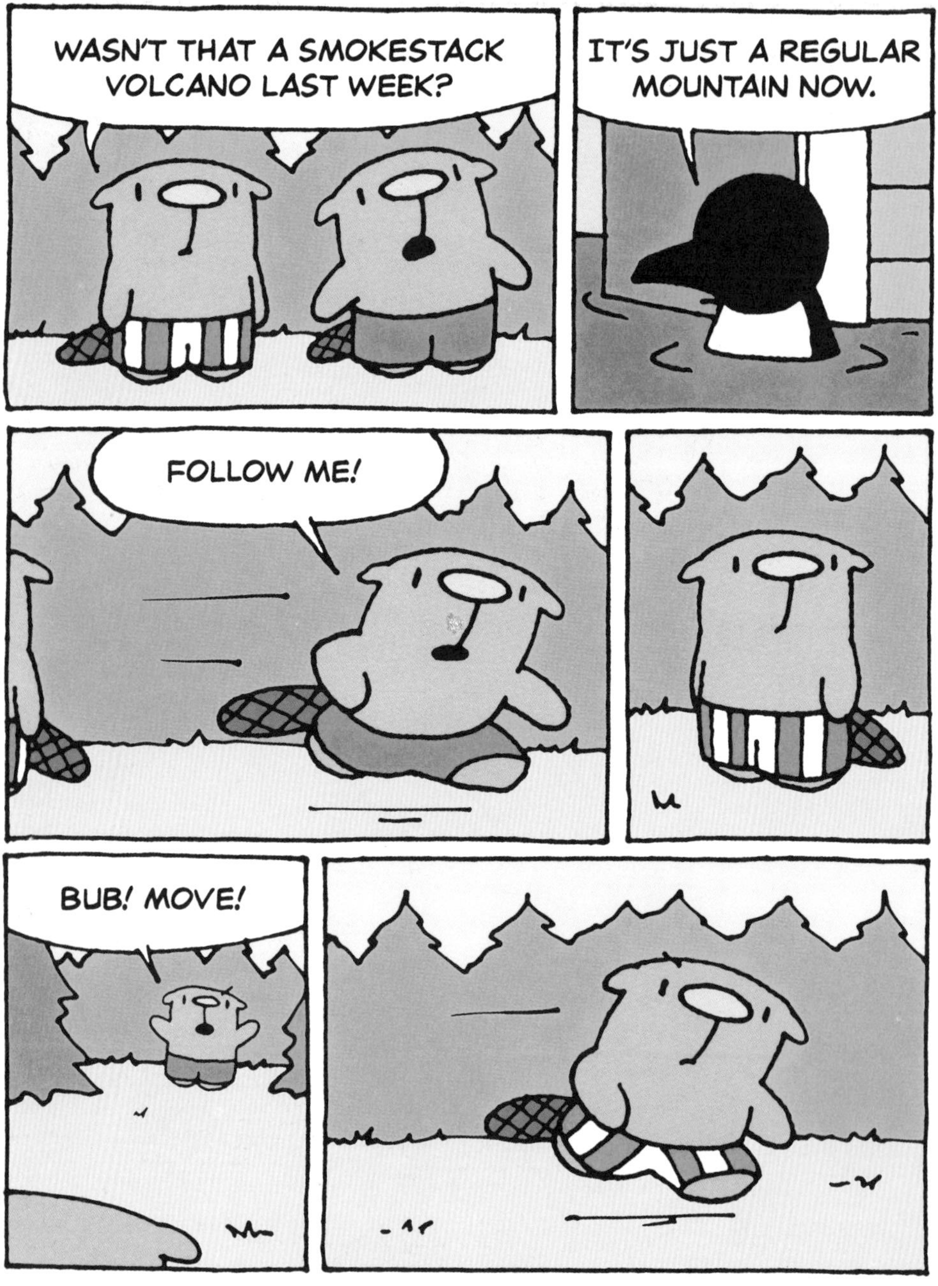
WASN'T THAT A SMOKESTACK VOLCANO LAST WEEK?
IT'S JUST A REGULAR MOUNTAIN NOW.
FOLLOW ME!
BUB! MOVE!

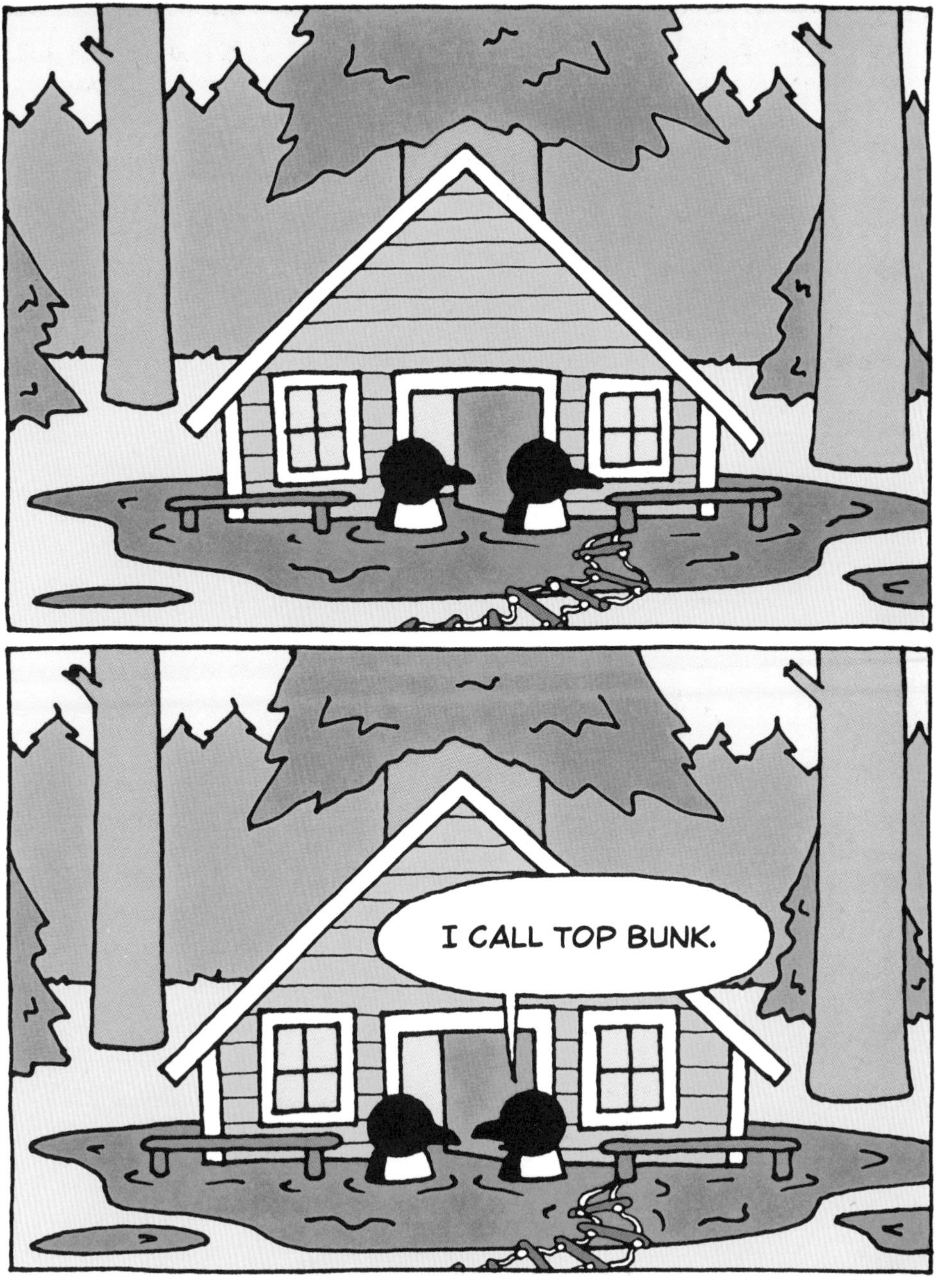
I CALL TOP BUNK.

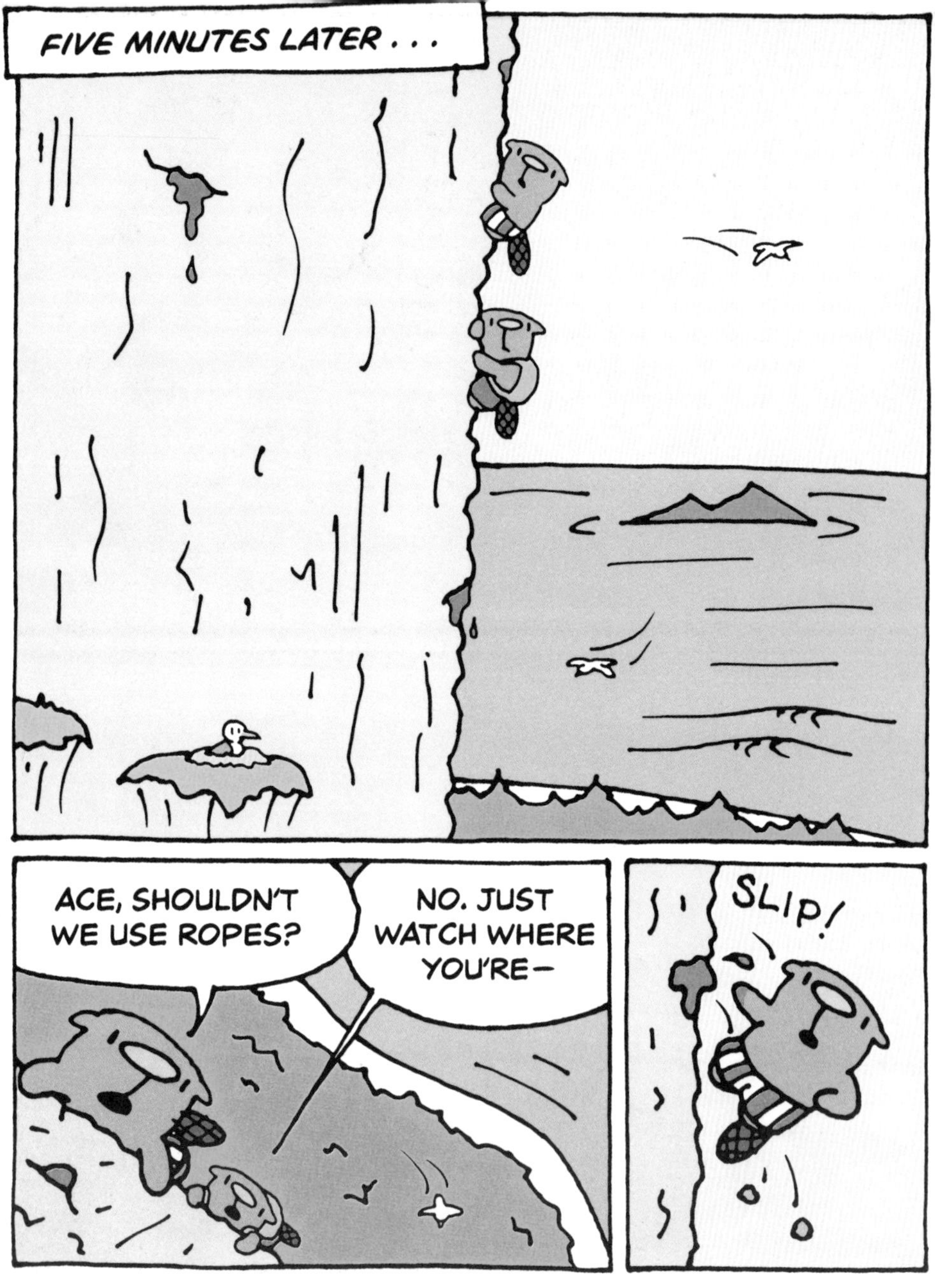
FIVE MINUTES LATER . . .
ACE, SHOULDN'T WE USE ROPES?
NO. JUST WATCH WHERE YOU'RE—
SLIP!

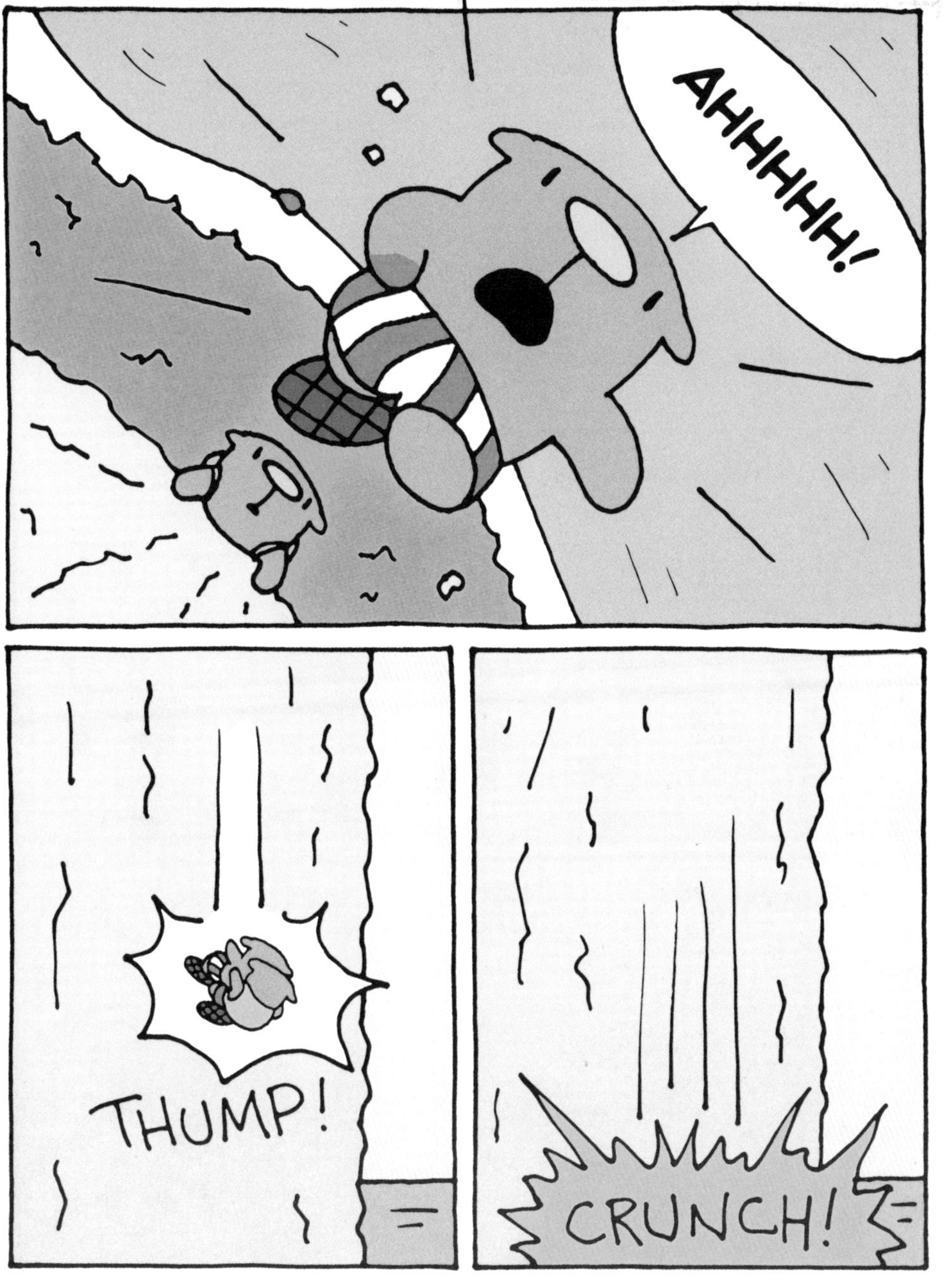
AHHHHH!
THUMP!
CRUNCH!

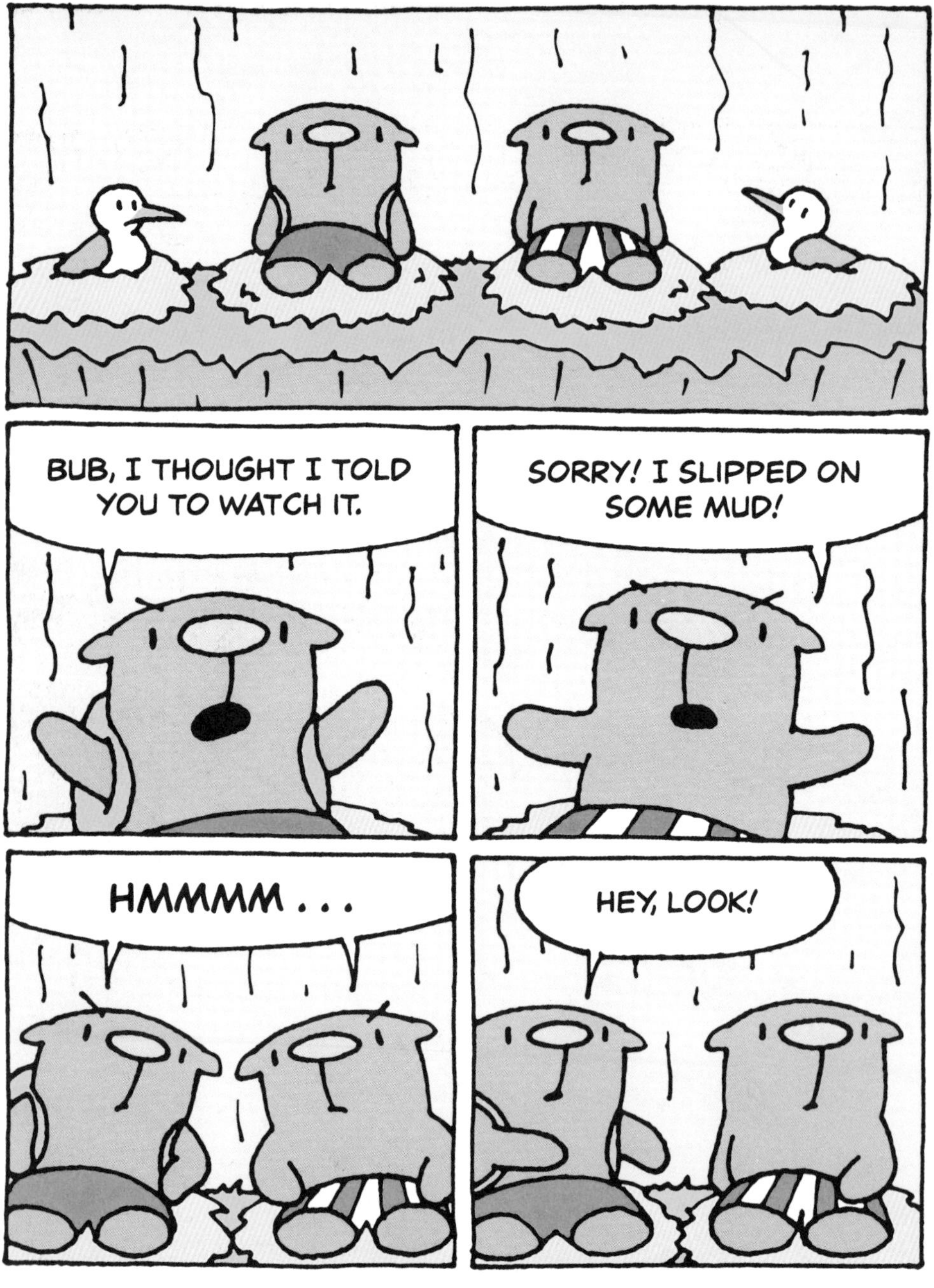
BUB, I THOUGHT I TOLD YOU TO WATCH IT.
SORRY! I SLIPPED ON SOME MUD!
HMMMM . . .
HEY, LOOK!

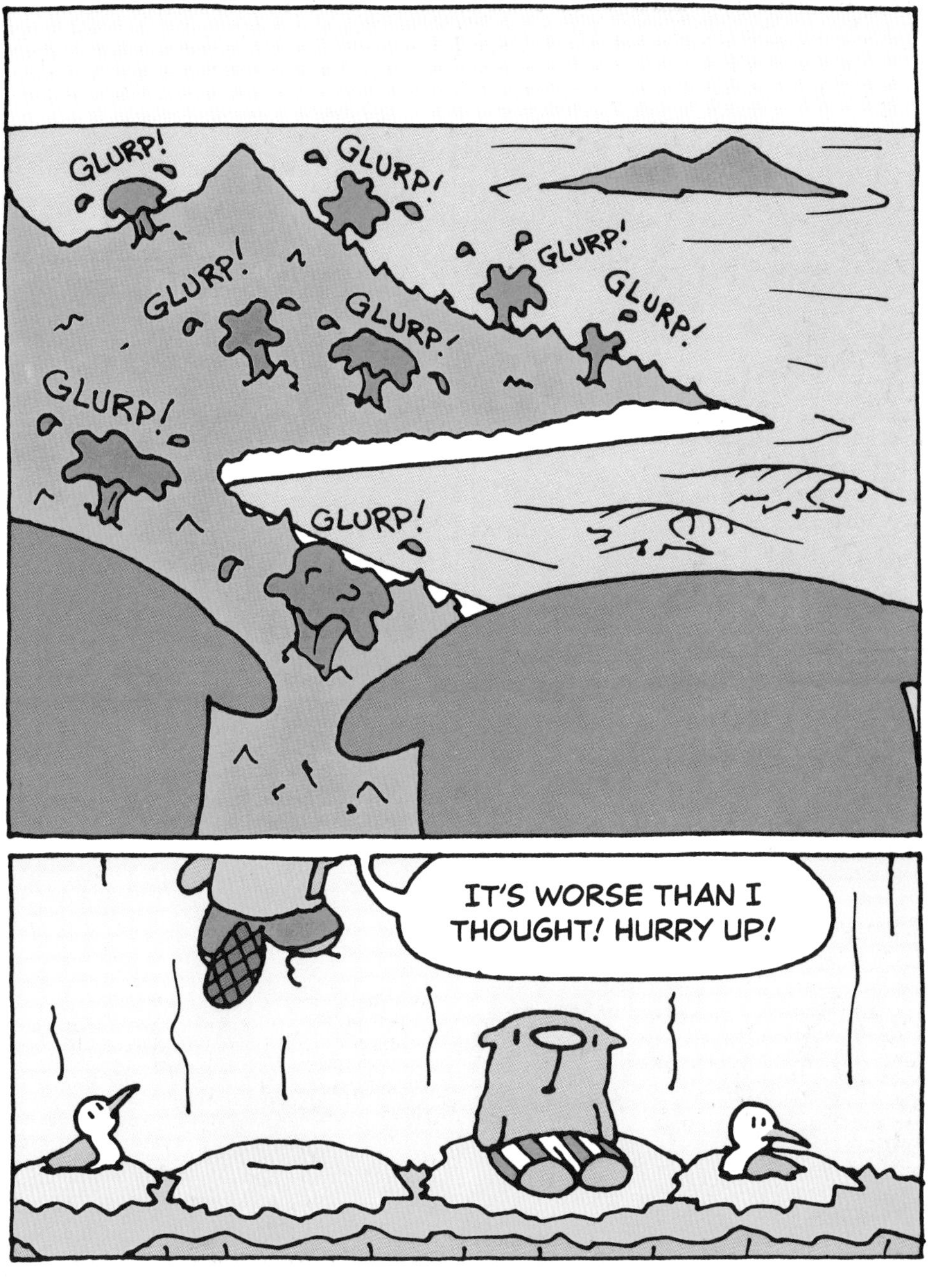
GLURP!
GLURP!
GLURP!
GLURP!
GLURP!
GLURP!
GLURP!
GLURP!
IT'S WORSE THAN I THOUGHT! HURRY UP!

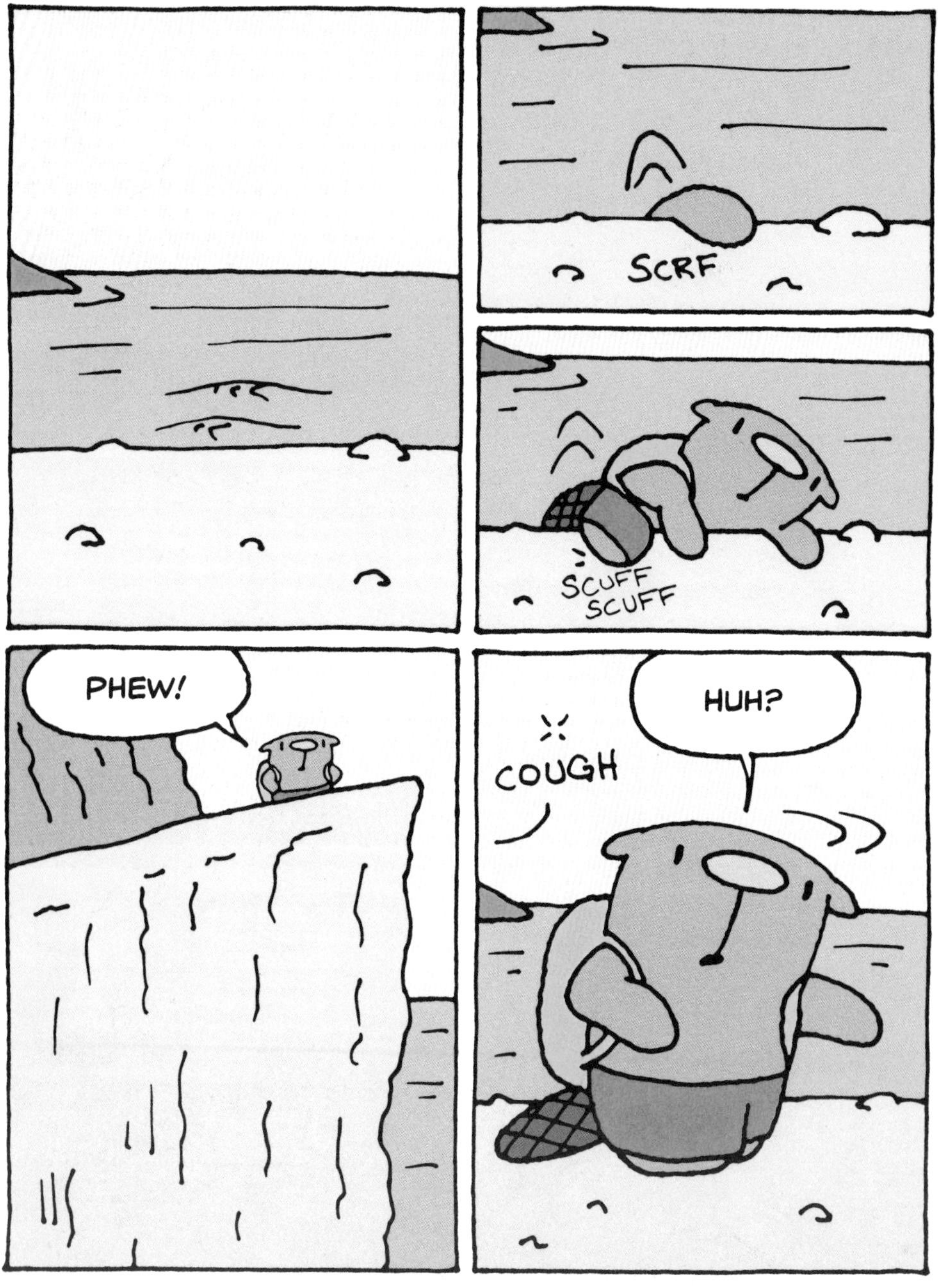
SCRF
SCUFF SCUFF
PHEW!
COUGH
HUH?

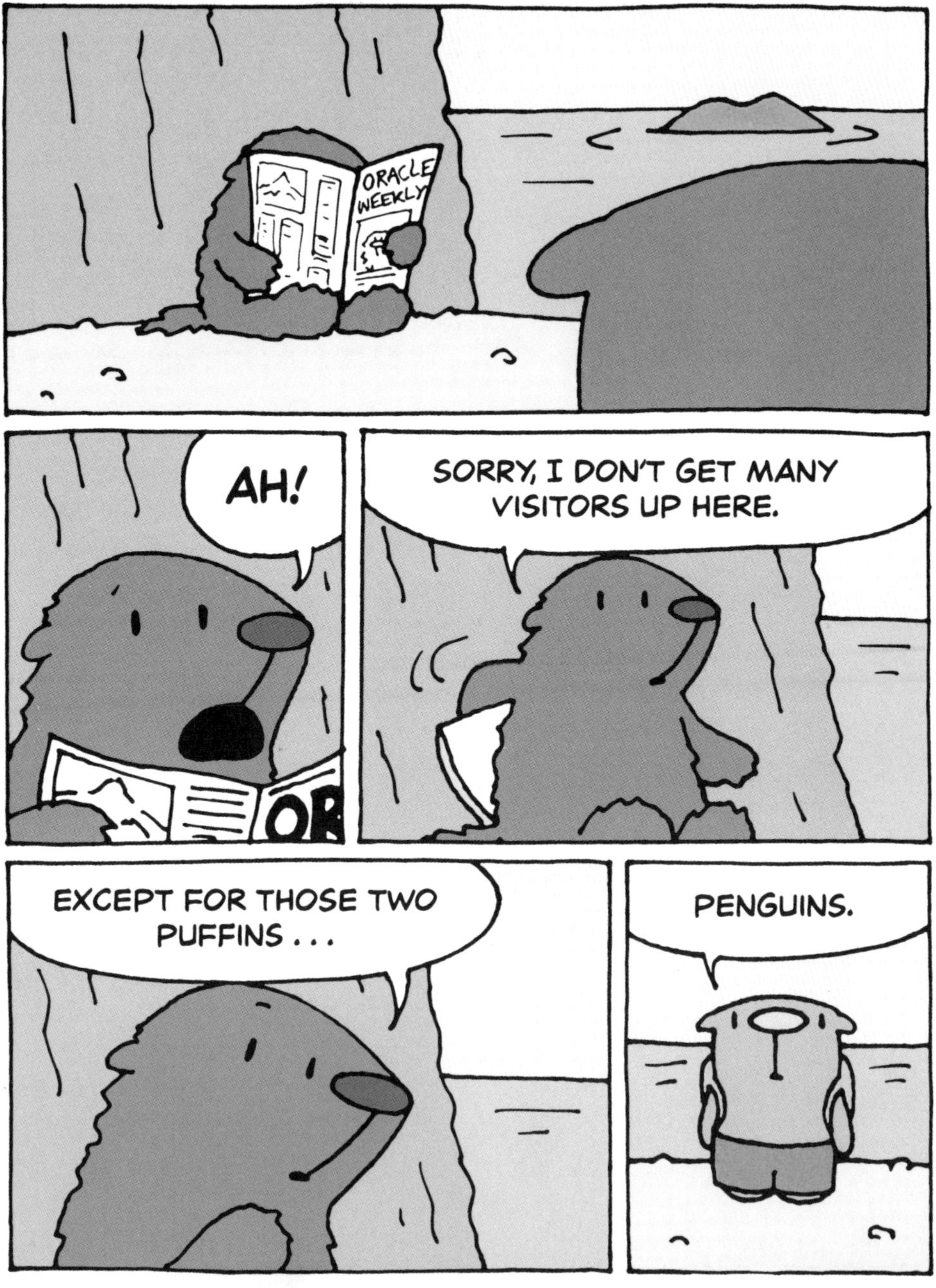
ORACLE WEEKLY
AH!
OR
SORRY, I DON'T GET MANY VISITORS UP HERE.
EXCEPT FOR THOSE TWO PUFFINS . . .
PENGUINS.

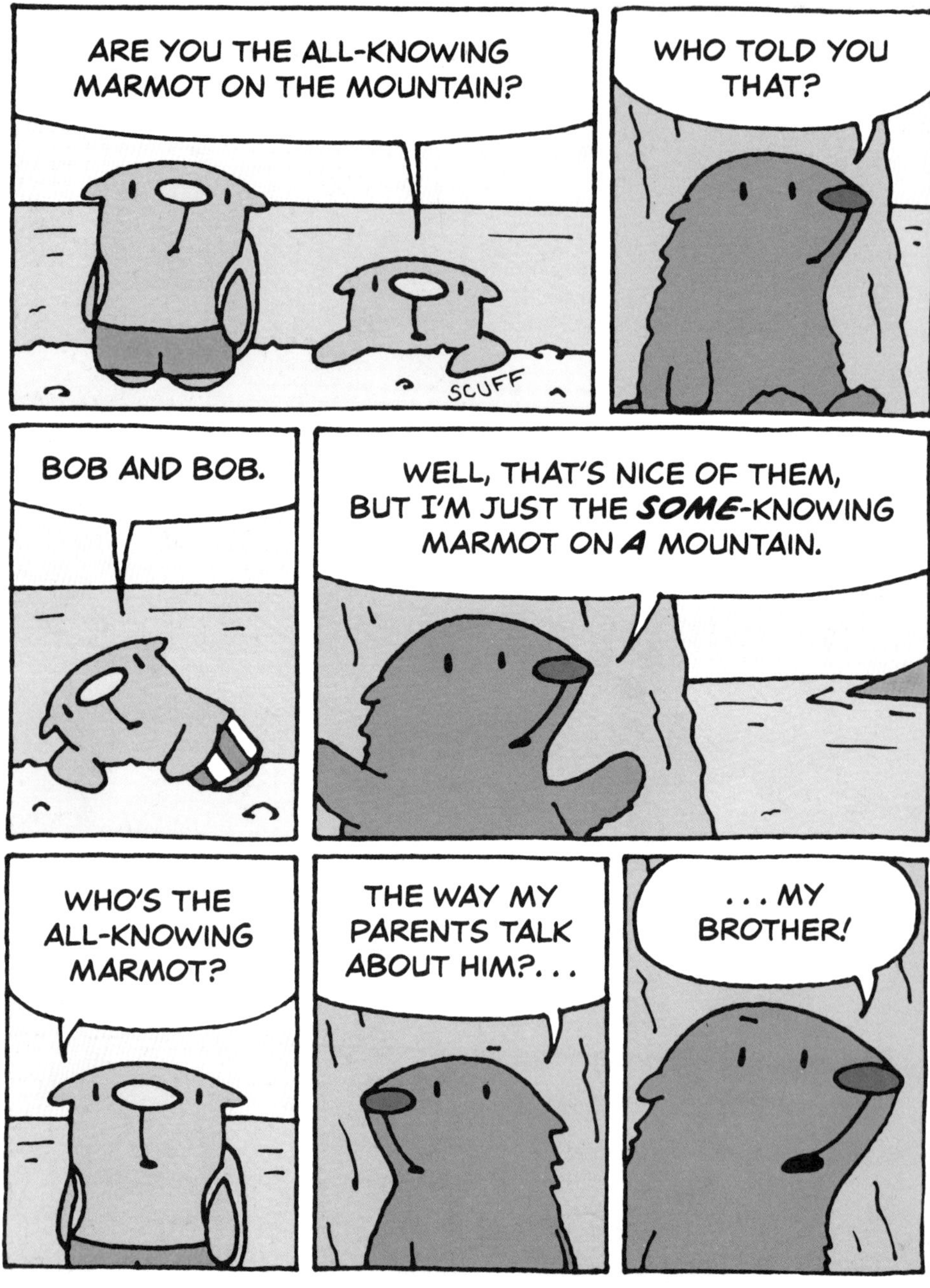
ARE YOU THE ALL-KNOWING MARMOT ON THE MOUNTAIN?
SCUFF
WHO TOLD YOU THAT?
BOB AND BOB.
WELL, THAT'S NICE OF THEM, BUT I'M JUST THE *SOME*-KNOWING MARMOT ON *A* MOUNTAIN.
WHO'S THE ALL-KNOWING MARMOT?
THE WAY MY PARENTS TALK ABOUT HIM?. . .
. . . MY BROTHER!

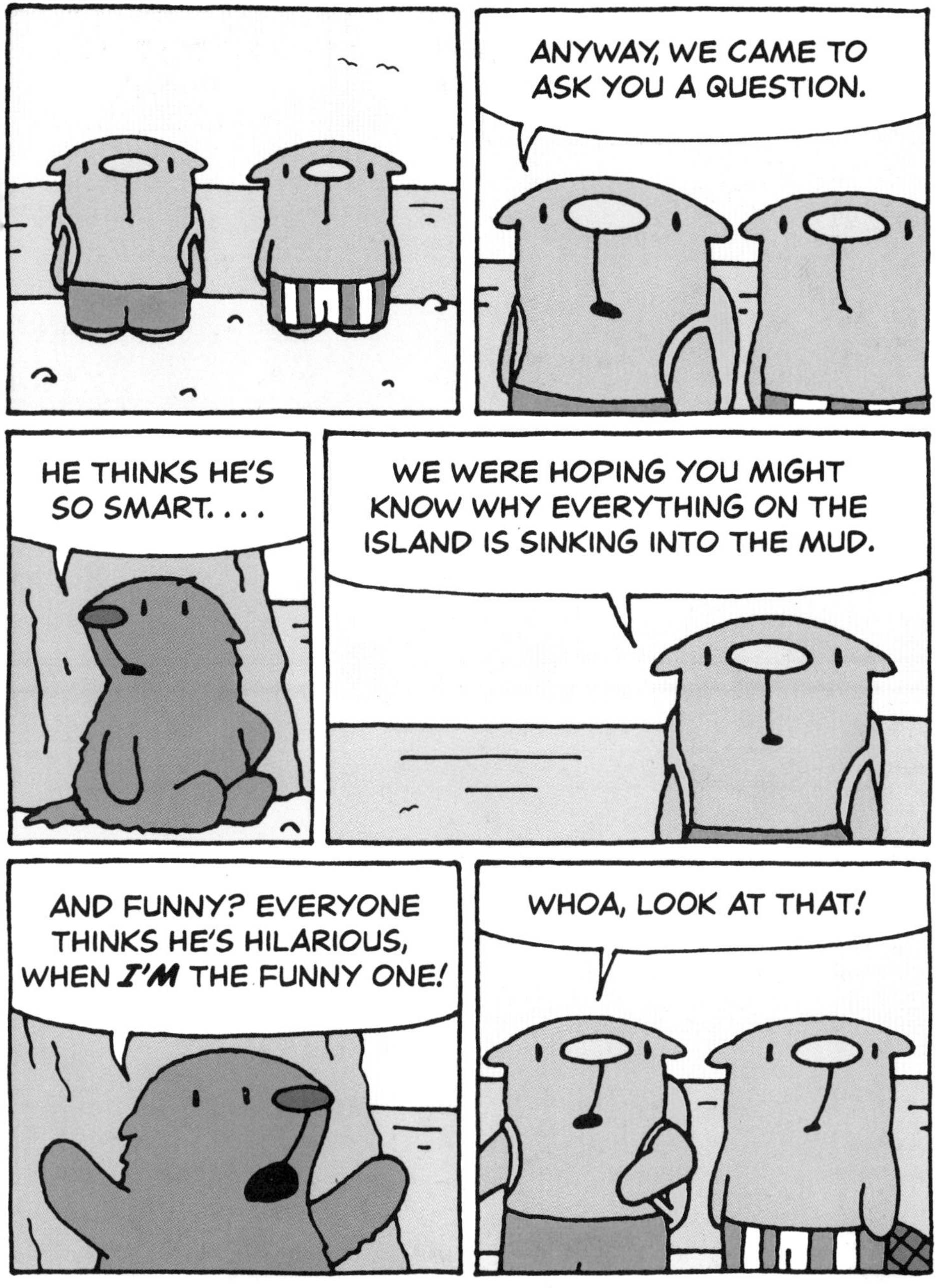
ANYWAY, WE CAME TO ASK YOU A QUESTION.
HE THINKS HE'S SO SMART. . . .
WE WERE HOPING YOU MIGHT KNOW WHY EVERYTHING ON THE ISLAND IS SINKING INTO THE MUD.
AND FUNNY? EVERYONE THINKS HE'S HILARIOUS, WHEN *I'M* THE FUNNY ONE!
WHOA, LOOK AT THAT!

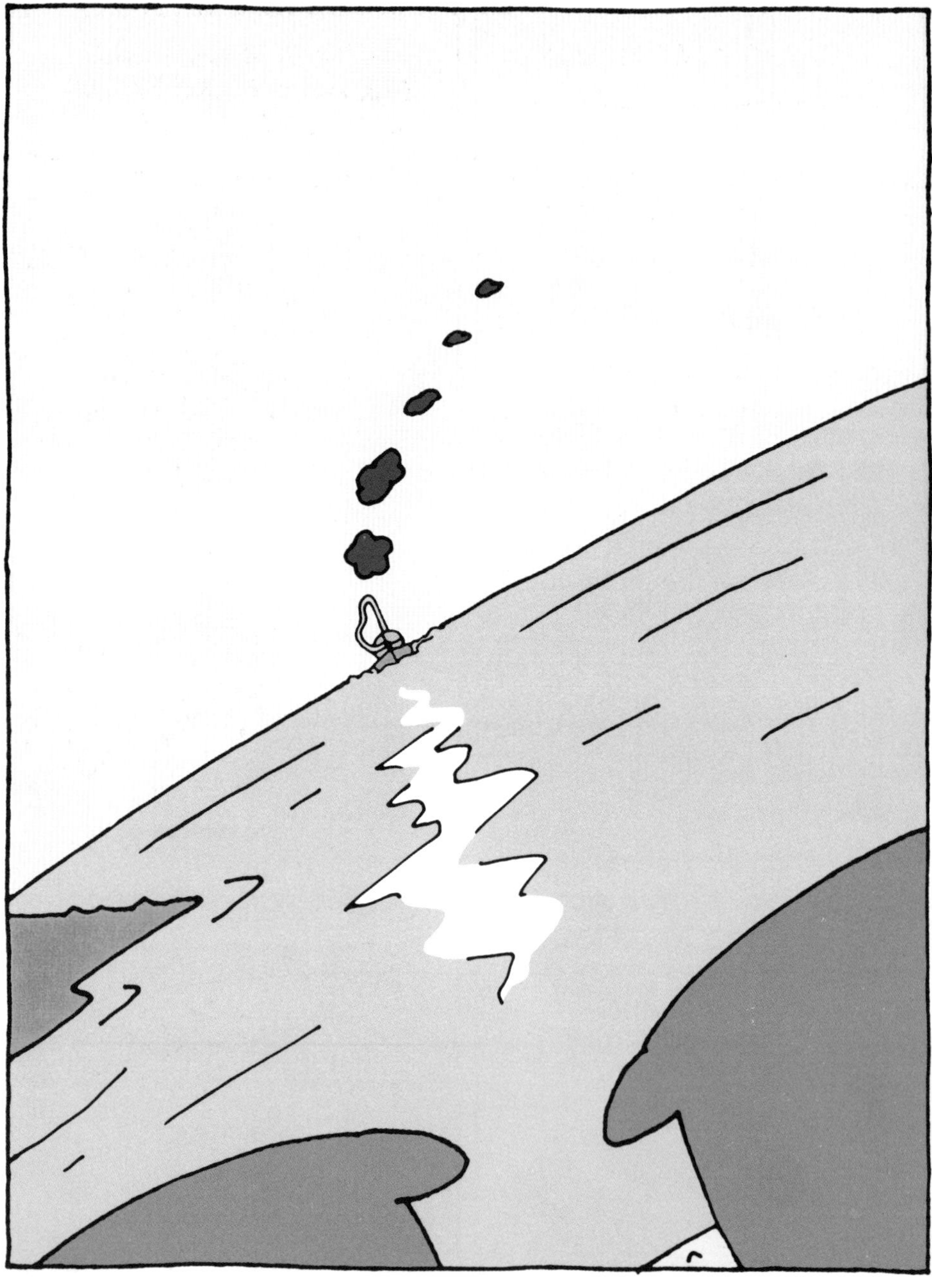

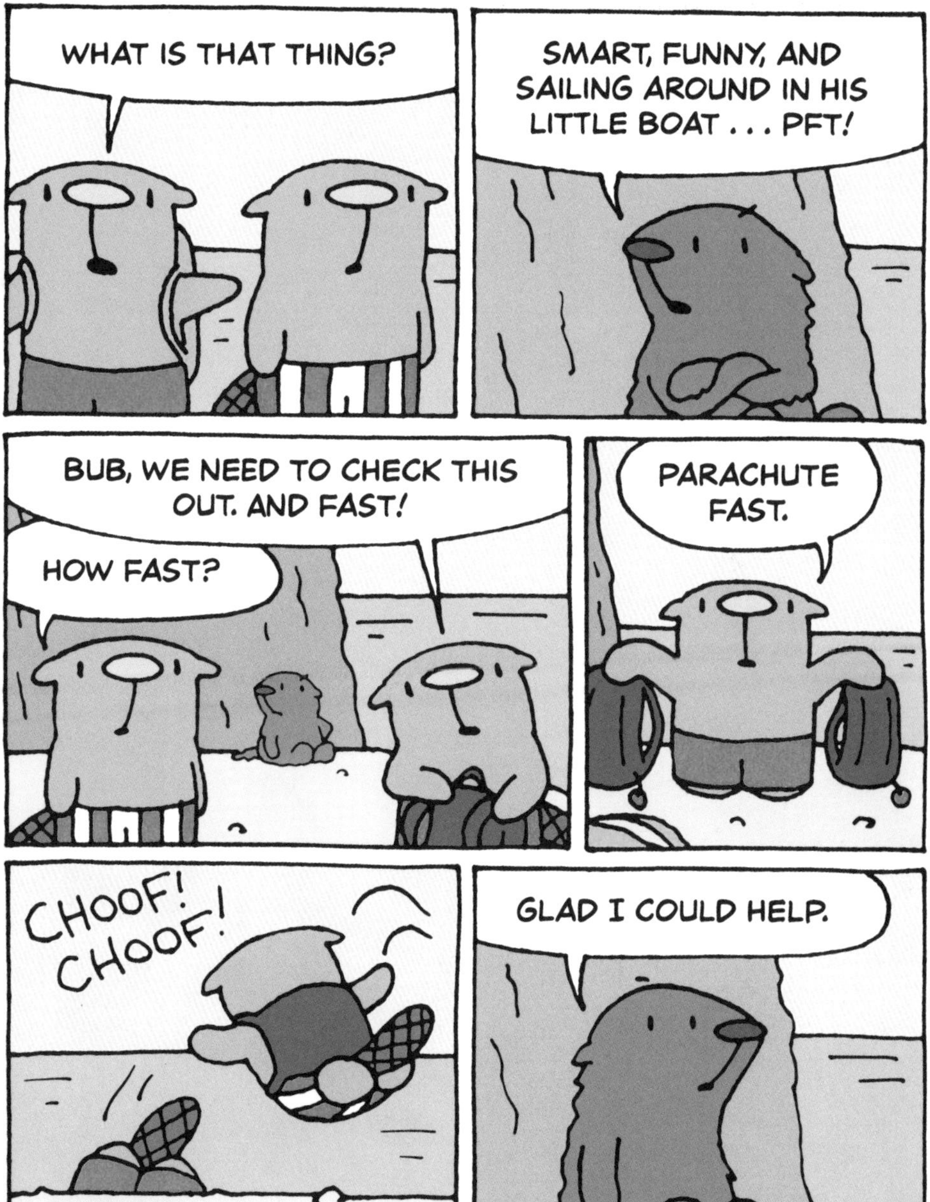
WHAT IS THAT THING?
SMART, FUNNY, AND SAILING AROUND IN HIS LITTLE BOAT . . . PFT!
BUB, WE NEED TO CHECK THIS OUT. AND FAST!
HOW FAST?
PARACHUTE FAST.
CHOOF! CHOOF!
GLAD I COULD HELP.

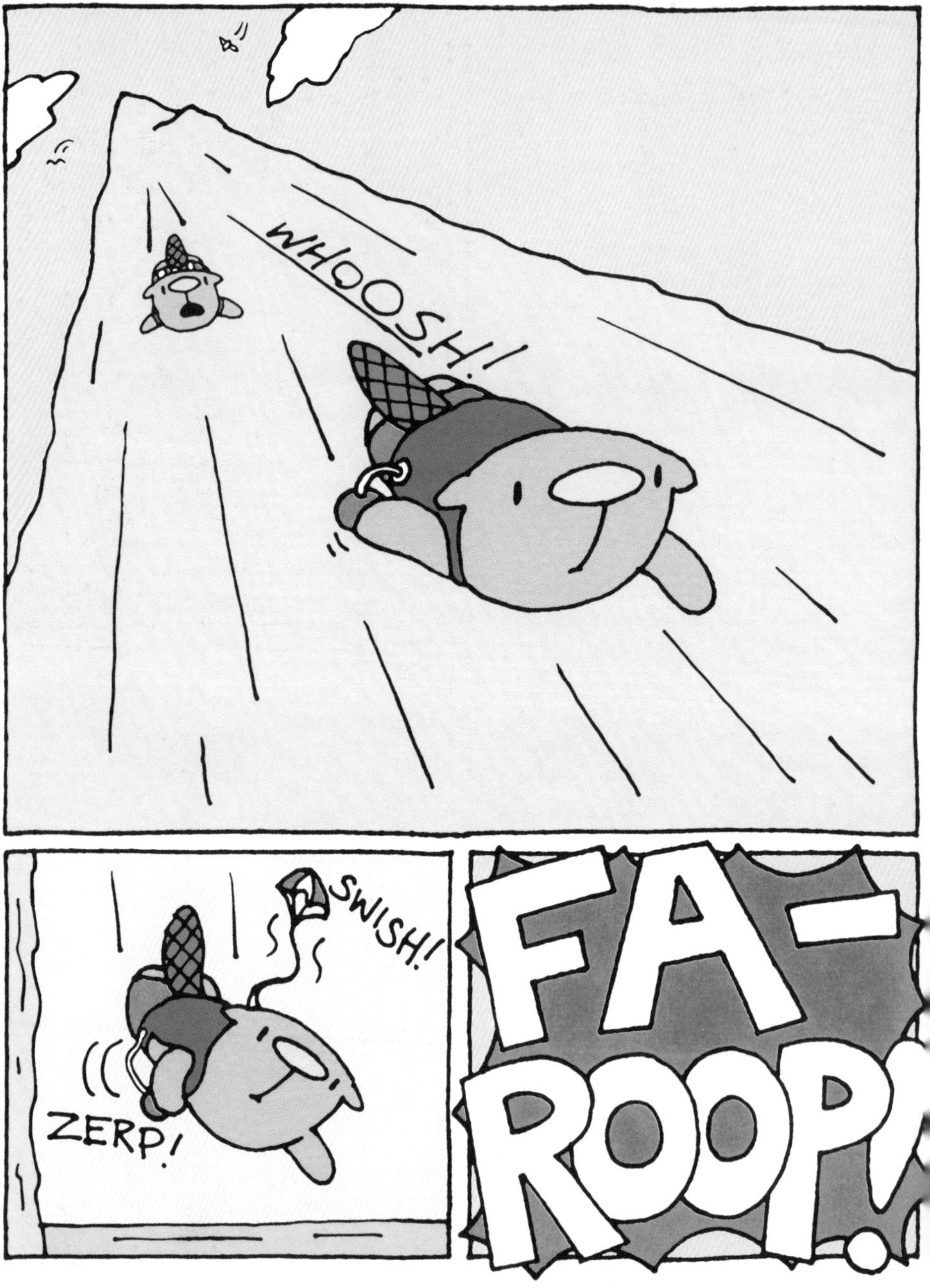
WHOOSH!!
SWISH!
ZERP!
FA-ROOP!

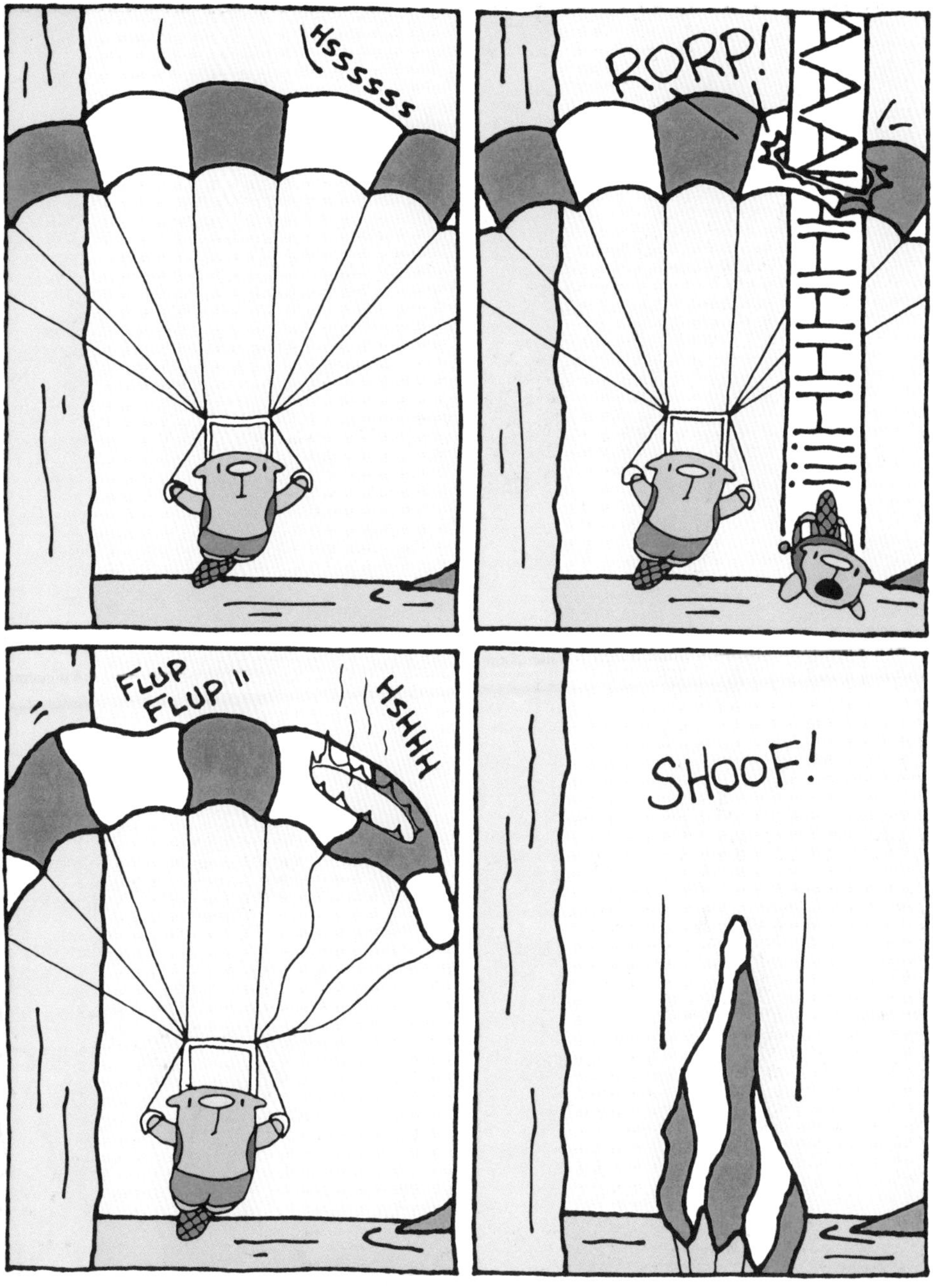
HSSSSSS
RORP!
AAAAHHHHHHH!!!
FLUP FLUP
HSHHH
SHOOF!

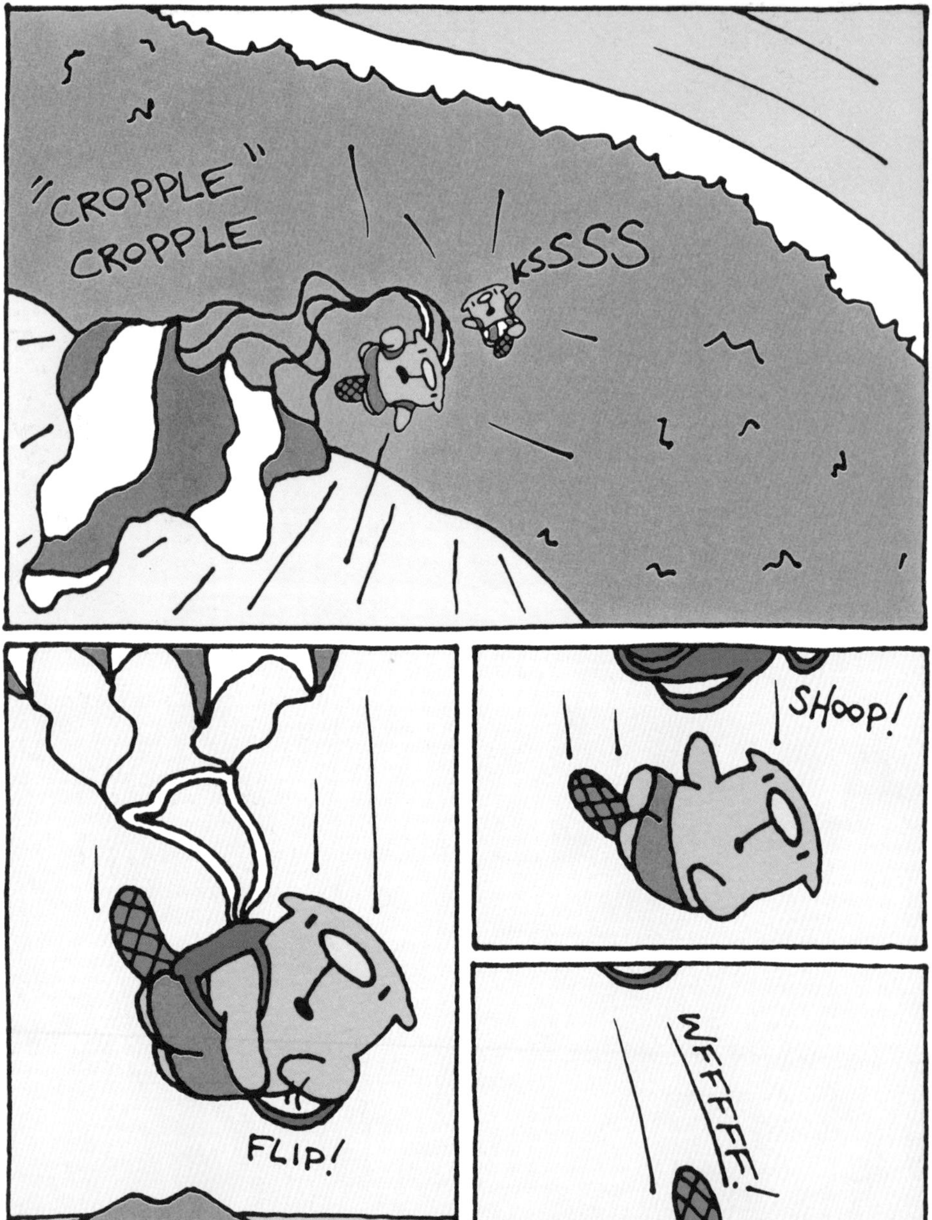
"CROPPLE
CROPPLE"
KSSSS
FLIP!
SHOOP!
WFFFFF!

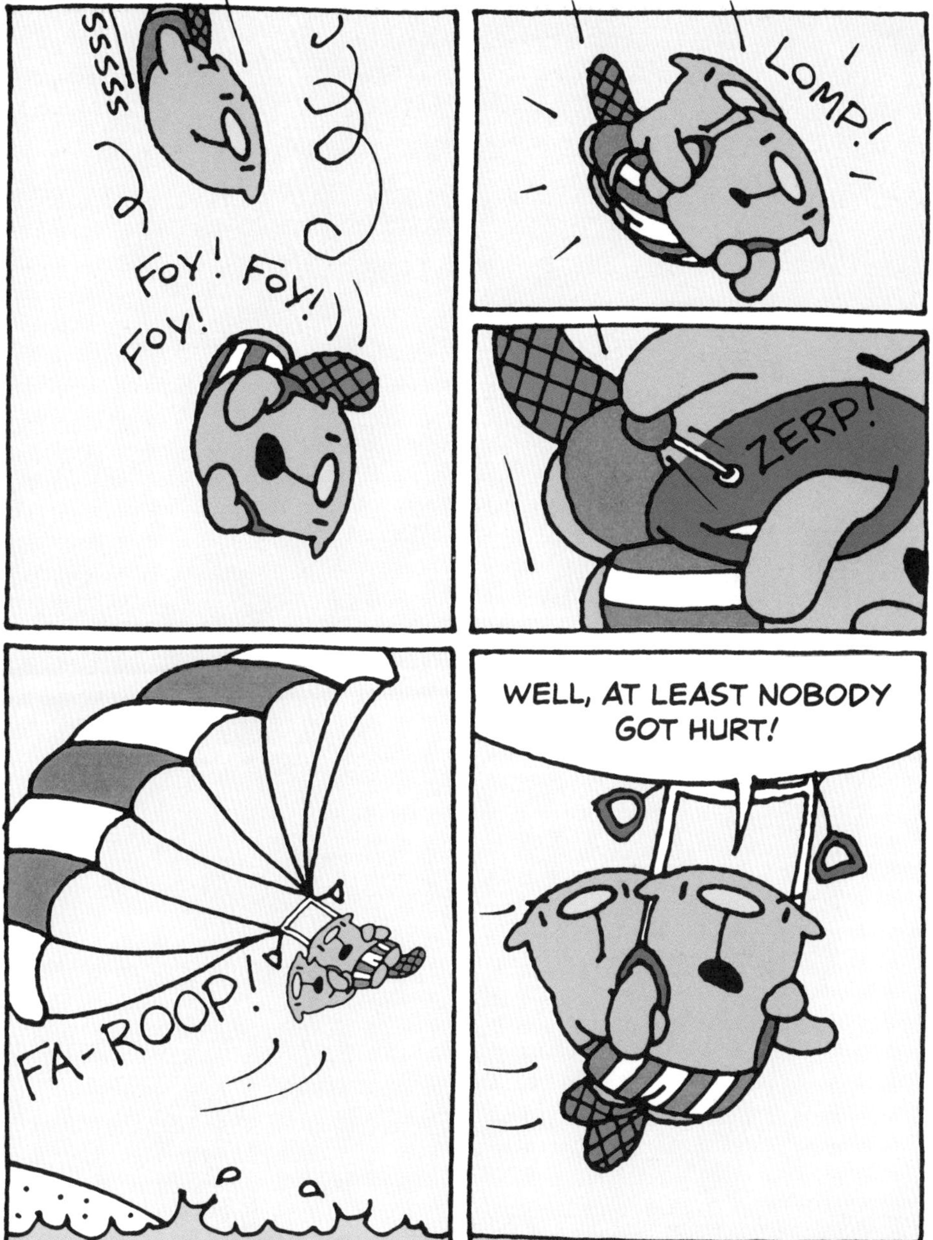
SSSSS
FOY! FOY! FOY!
LOMP!
ZERP!
FA-ROOP!
WELL, AT LEAST NOBODY GOT HURT!

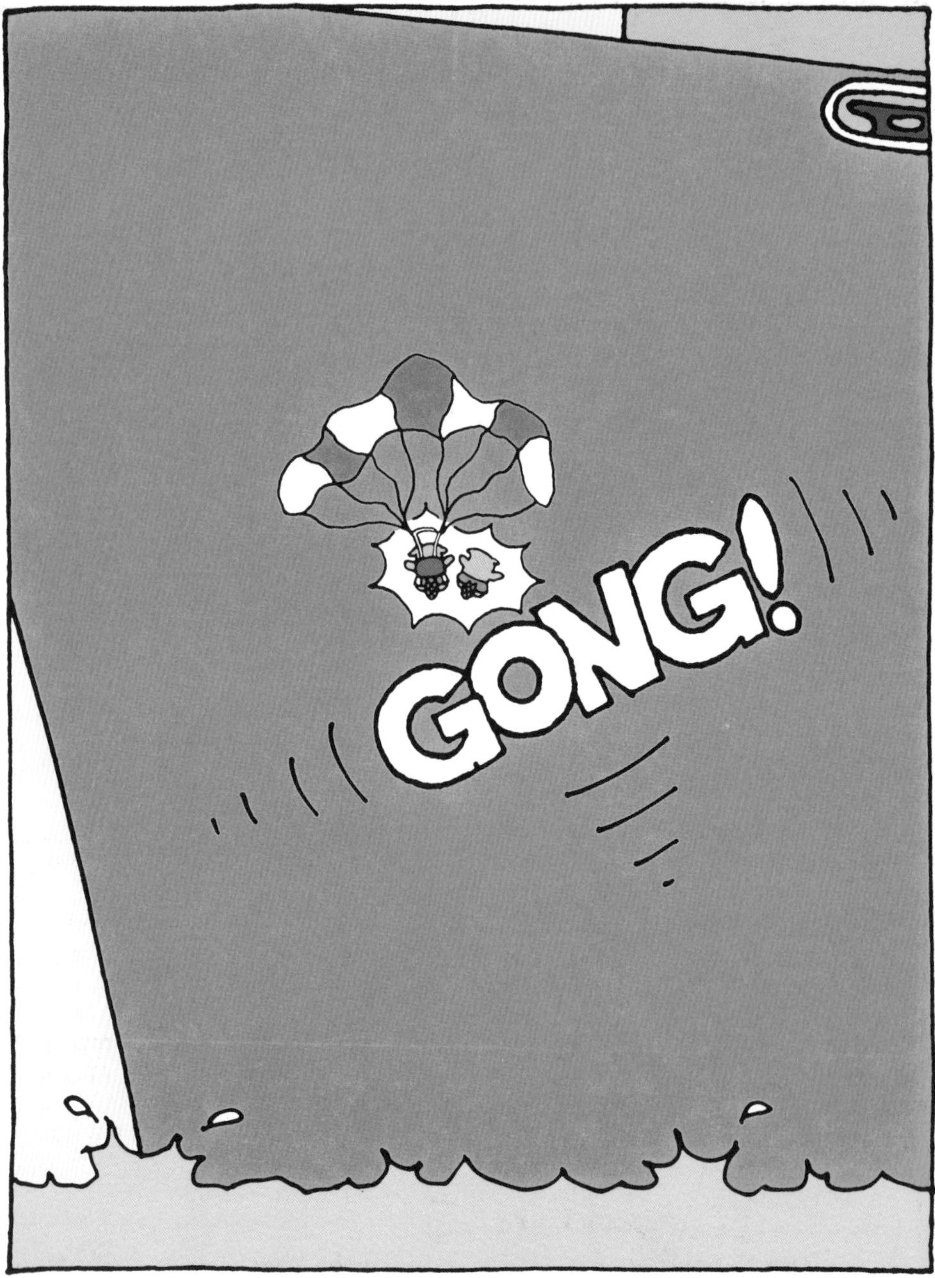
GONG!

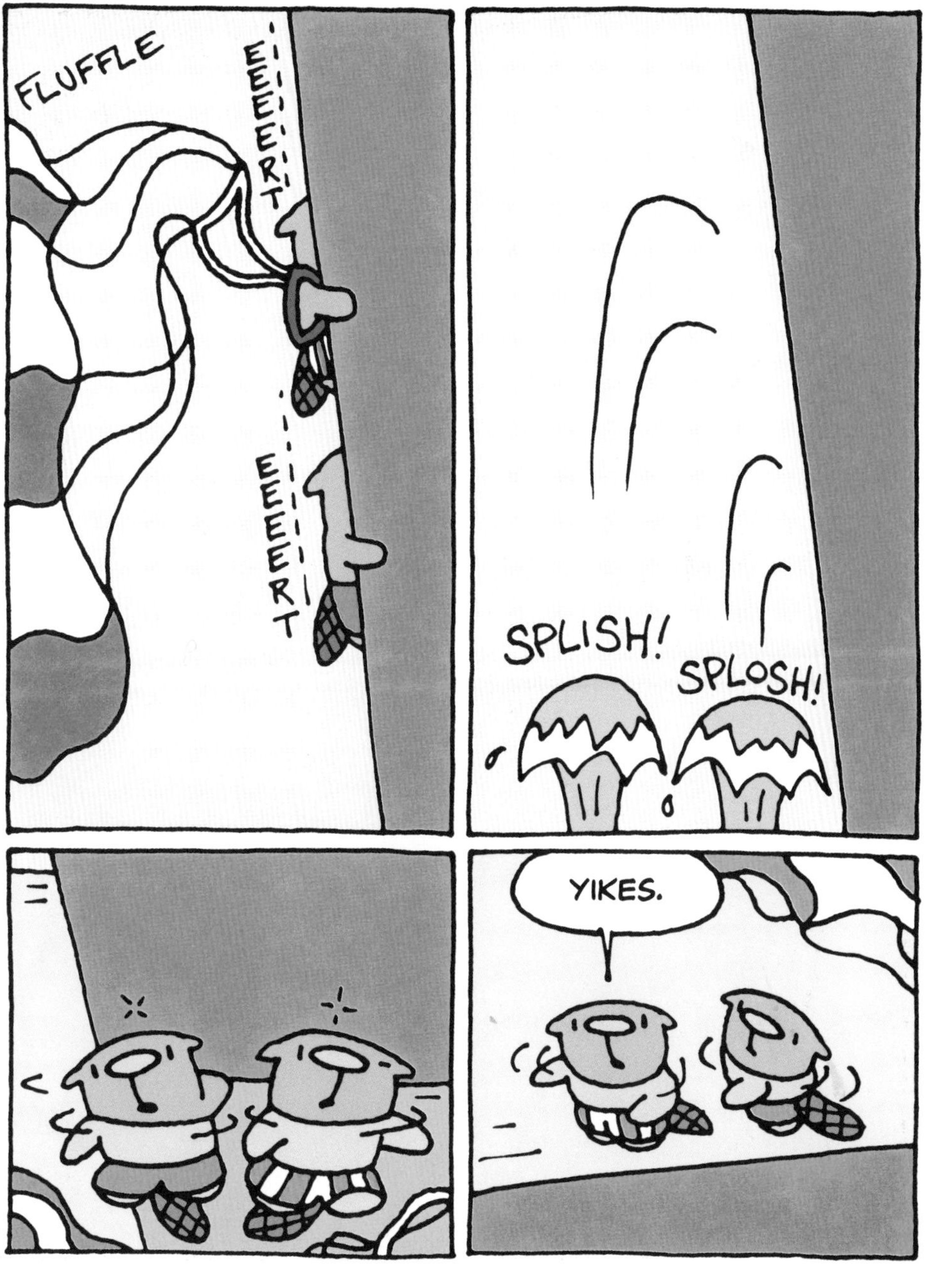
FLUFFLE
EEEEERT
EEEEERT
SPLISH!
SPLOSH!
YIKES.

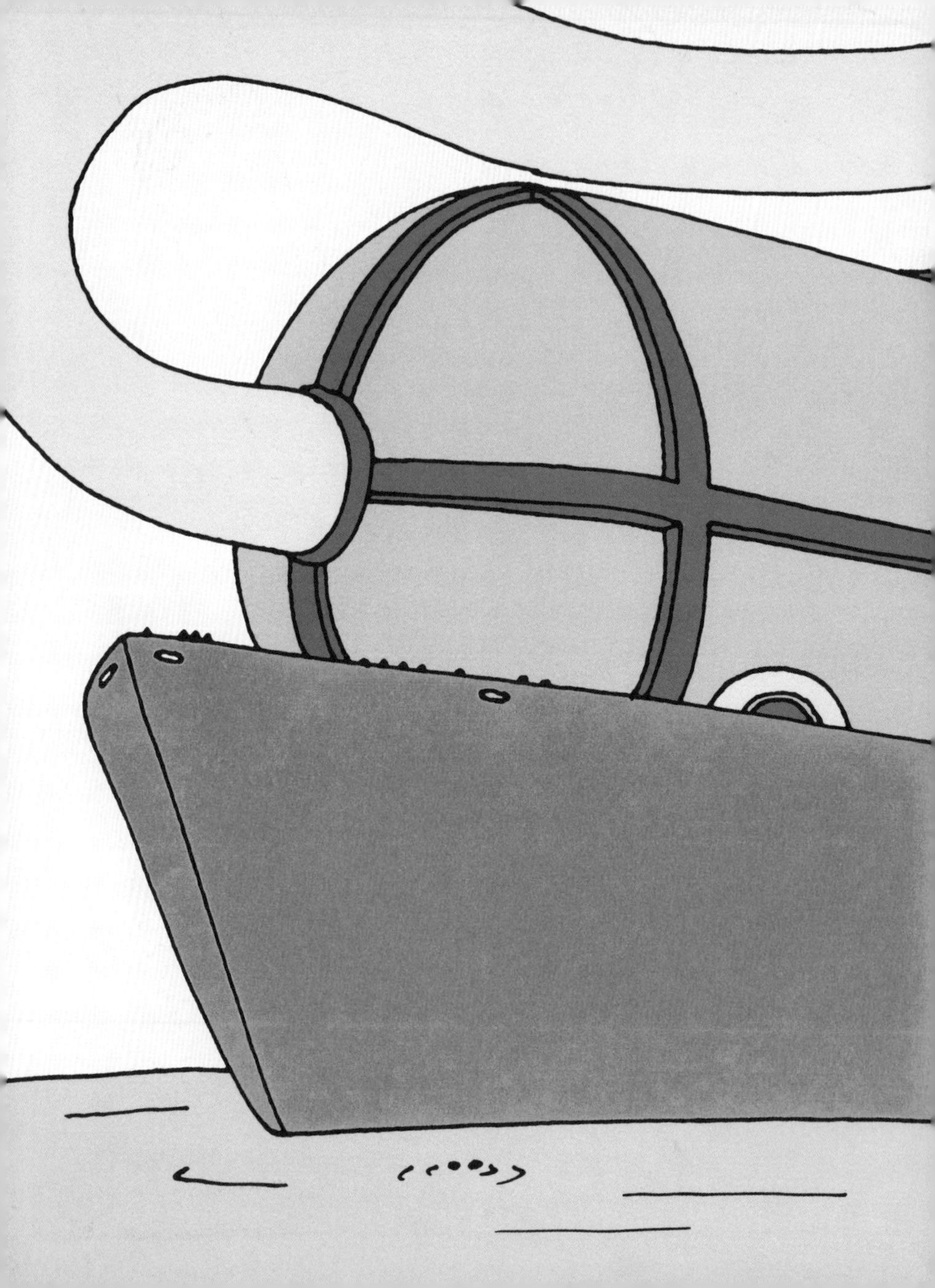

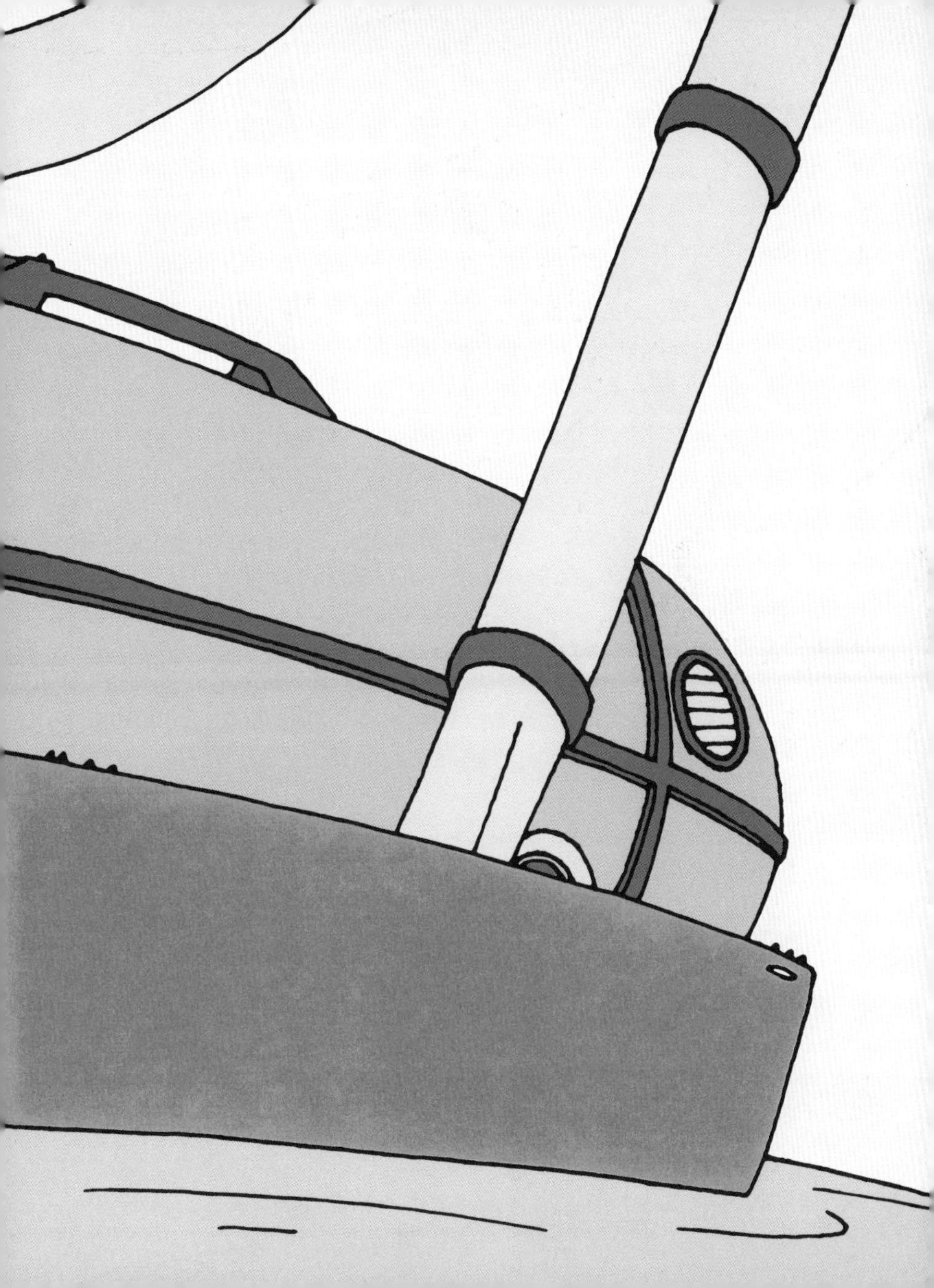

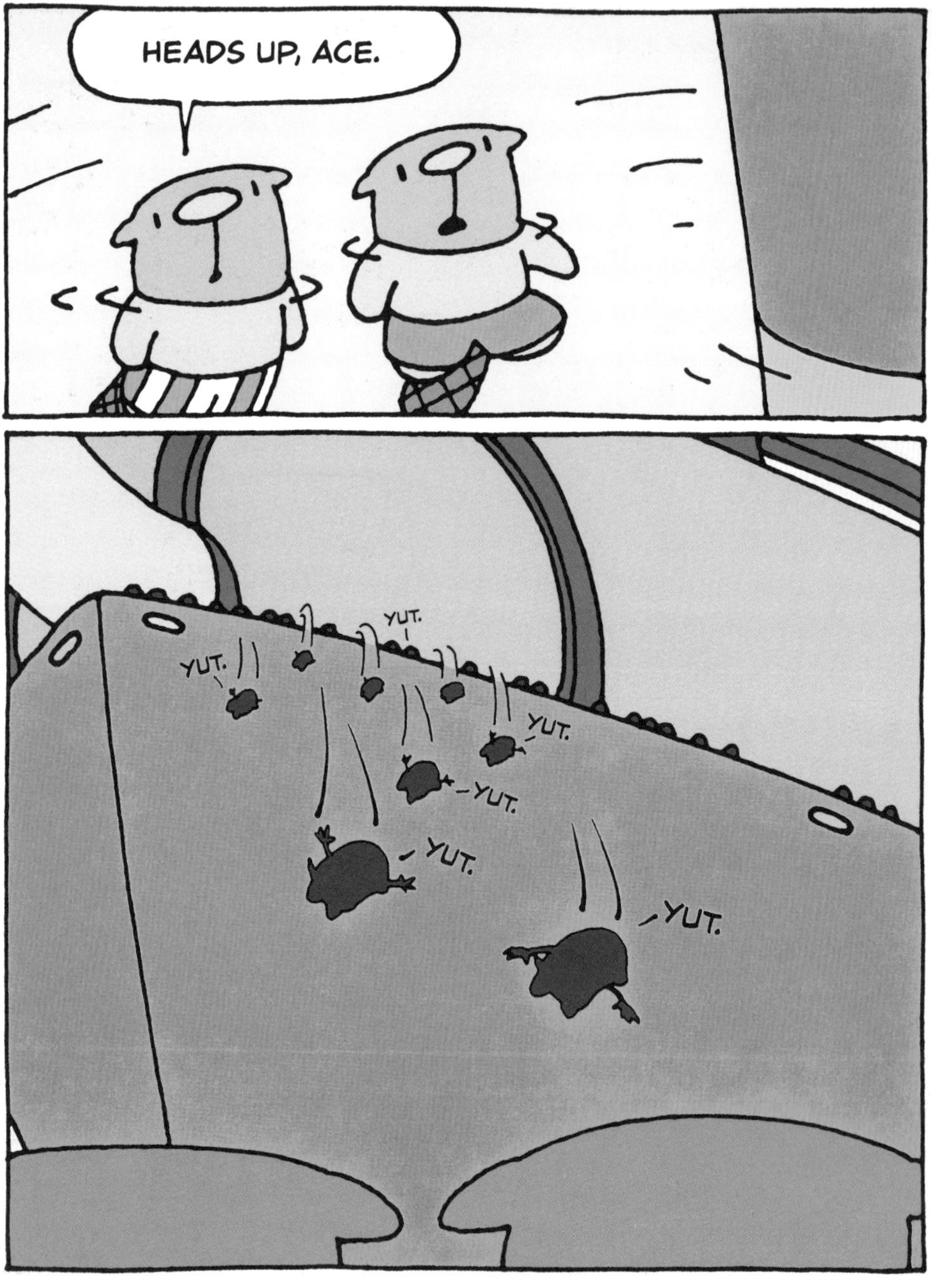
HEADS UP, ACE.
YUT.
YUT.
YUT.
YUT.
YUT.
YUT.

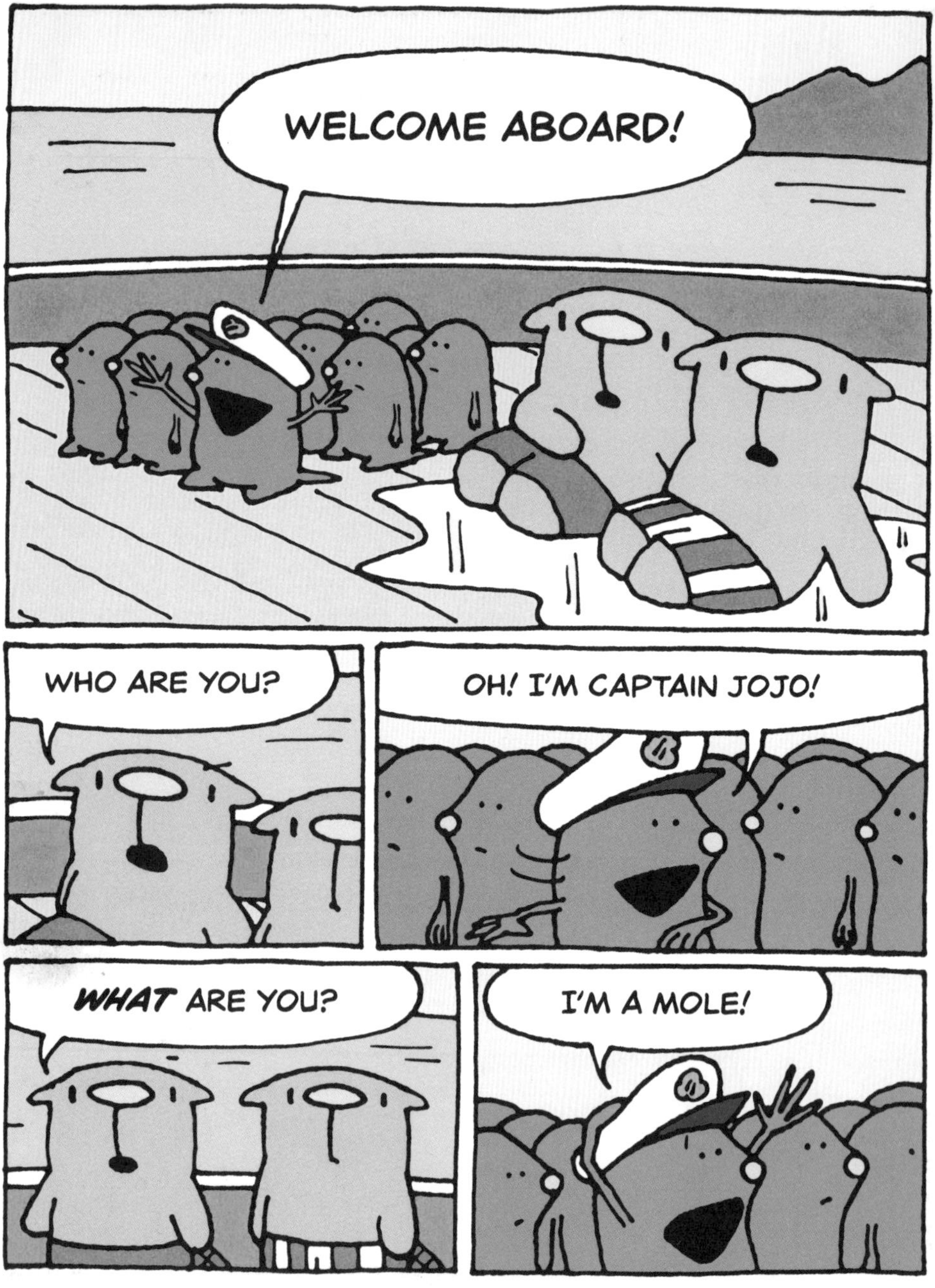
WELCOME ABOARD!
WHO ARE YOU?
OH! I'M CAPTAIN JOJO!
WHAT ARE YOU?
I'M A MOLE!

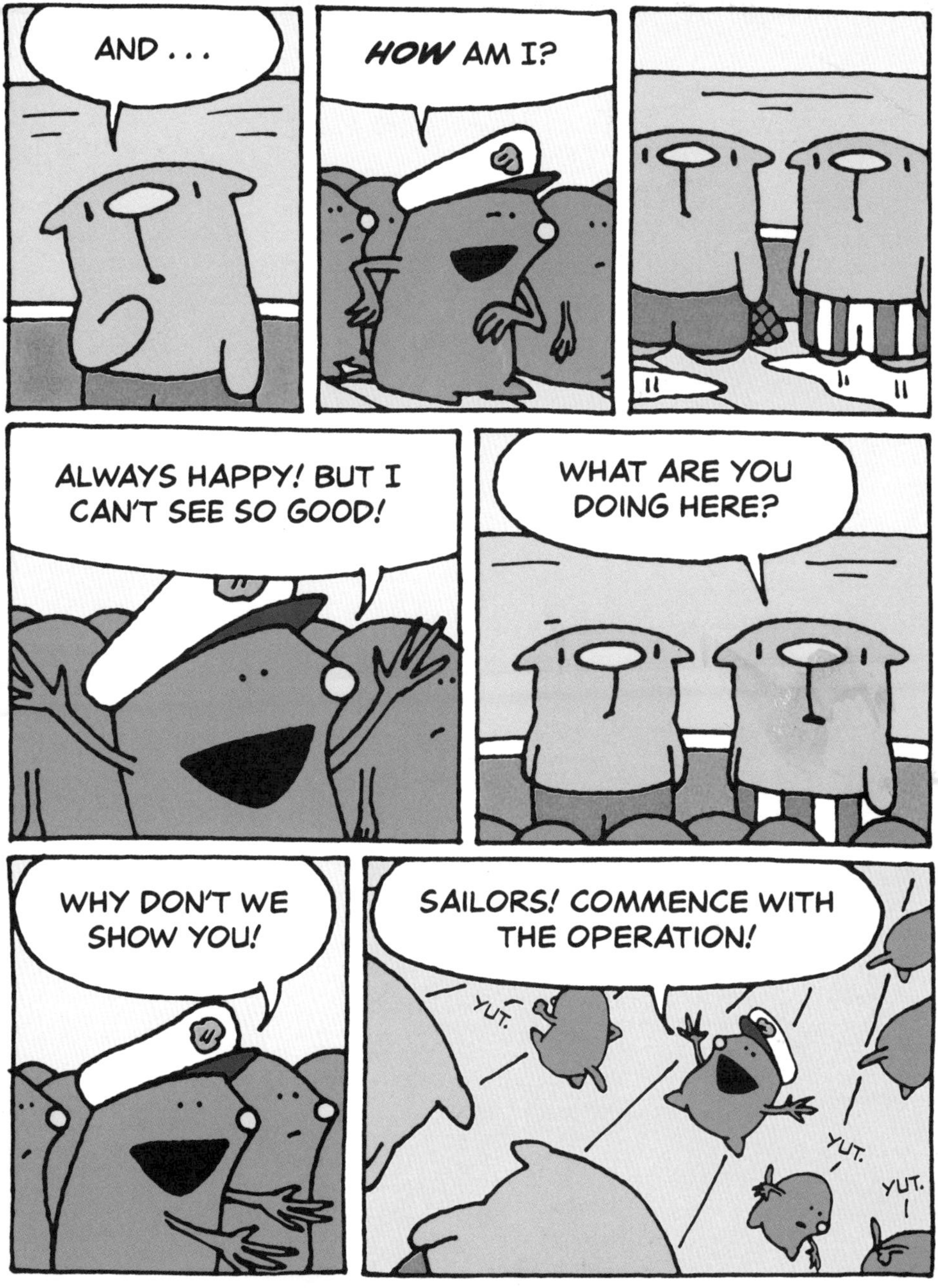
AND . . .
HOW AM I?
ALWAYS HAPPY! BUT I CAN'T SEE SO GOOD!
WHAT ARE YOU DOING HERE?
WHY DON'T WE SHOW YOU!
SAILORS! COMMENCE WITH THE OPERATION!
YUT.
YUT.
YUT.

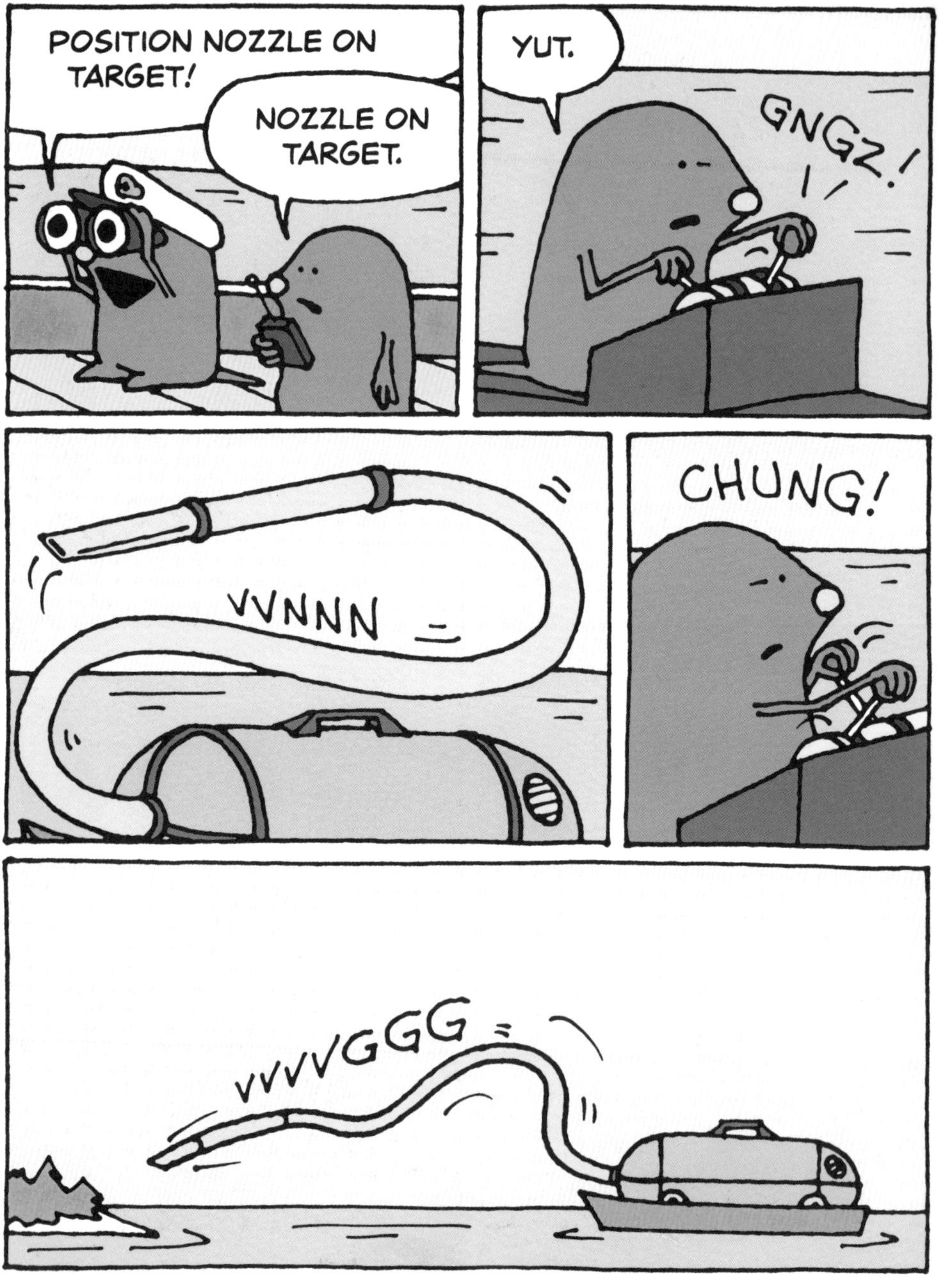
POSITION NOZZLE ON TARGET!
NOZZLE ON TARGET.
YUT.
GNGZ!
VVNNN
CHUNG!
VVVVGGG

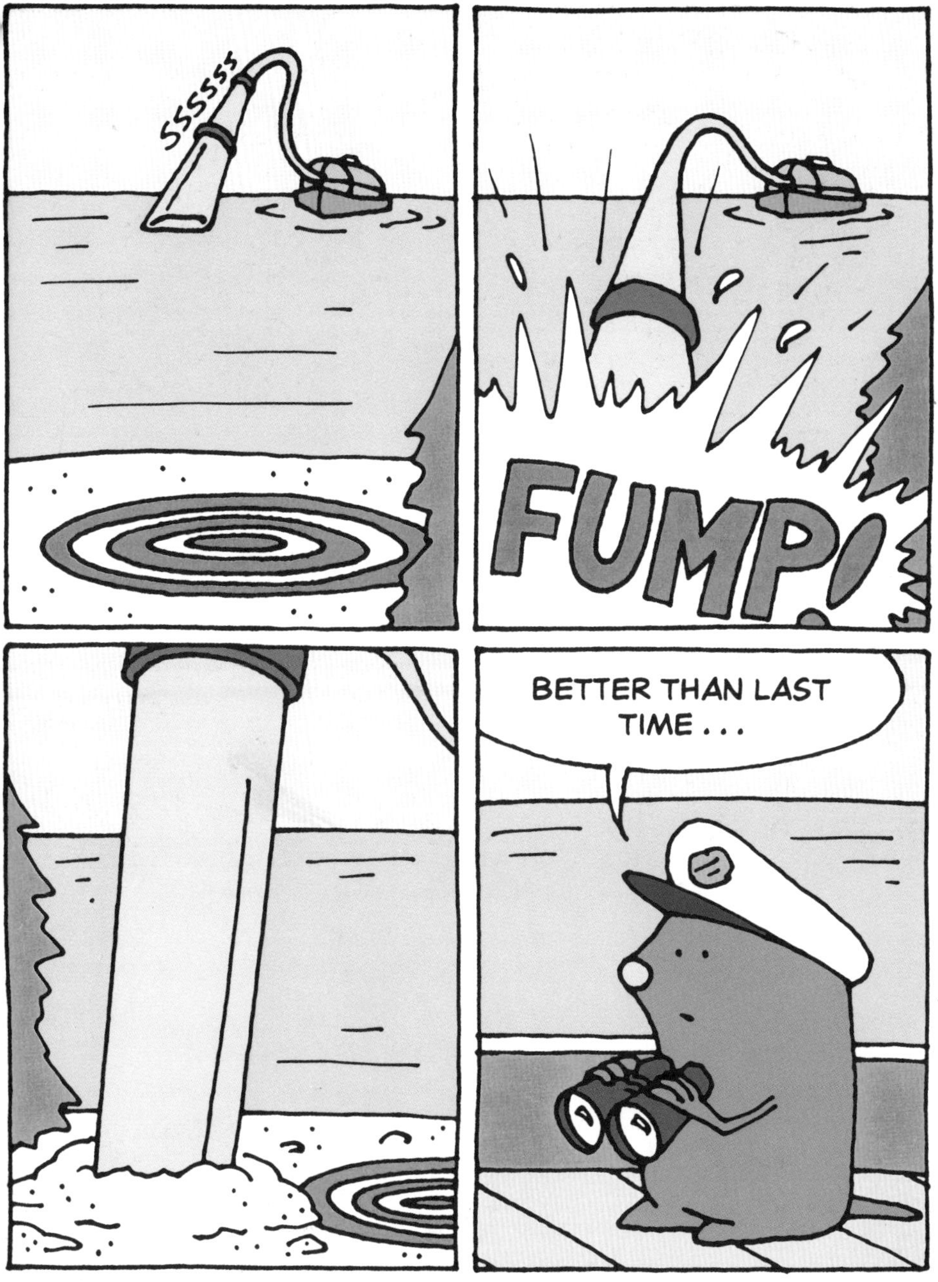
SSSSSS
FUMP!
BETTER THAN LAST TIME . . .

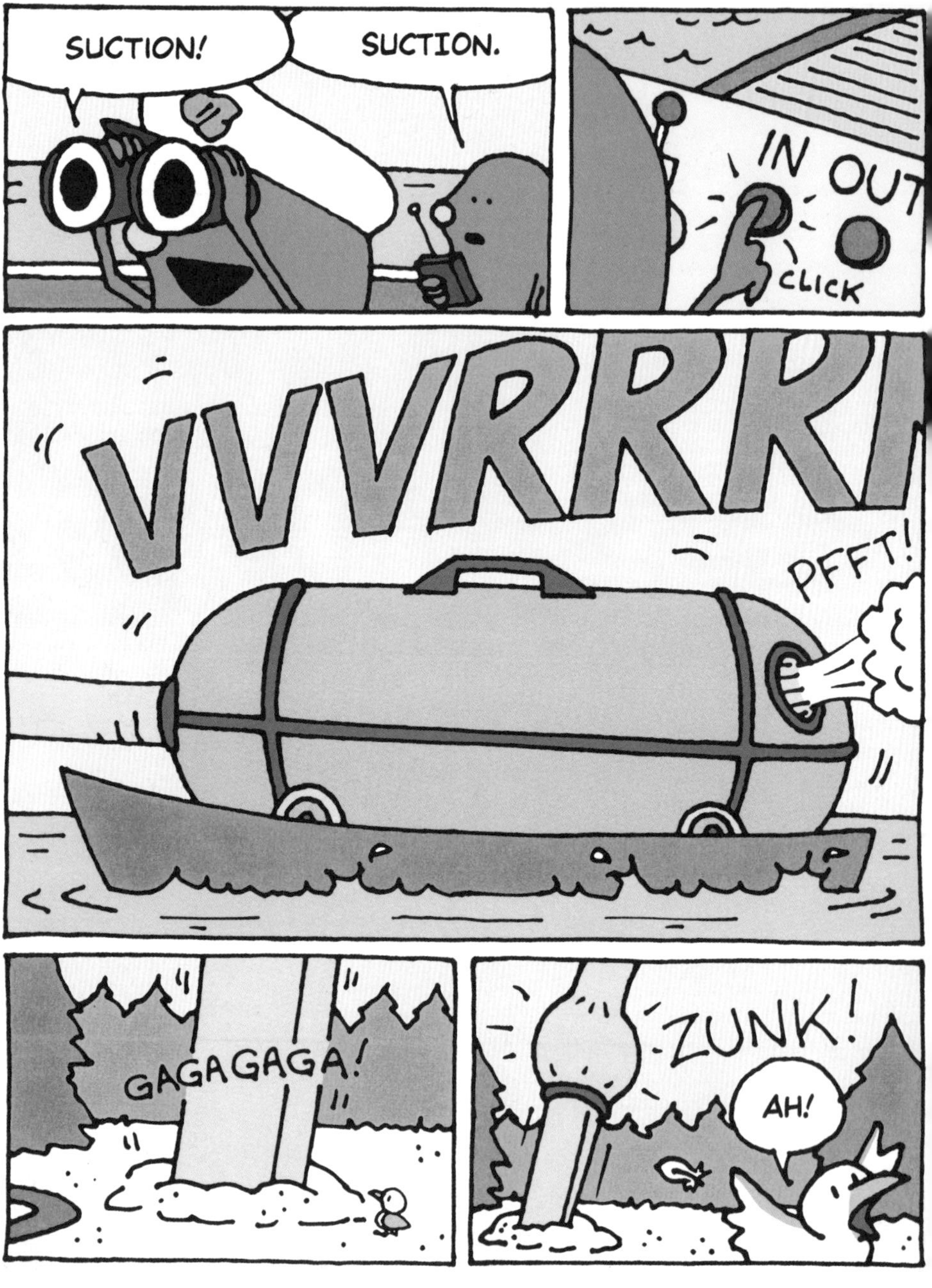
SUCTION!
SUCTION.
IN
OUT
CLICK
VVVRRRR
PFFT!
GAGAGAGA!
ZUNK!
AH!

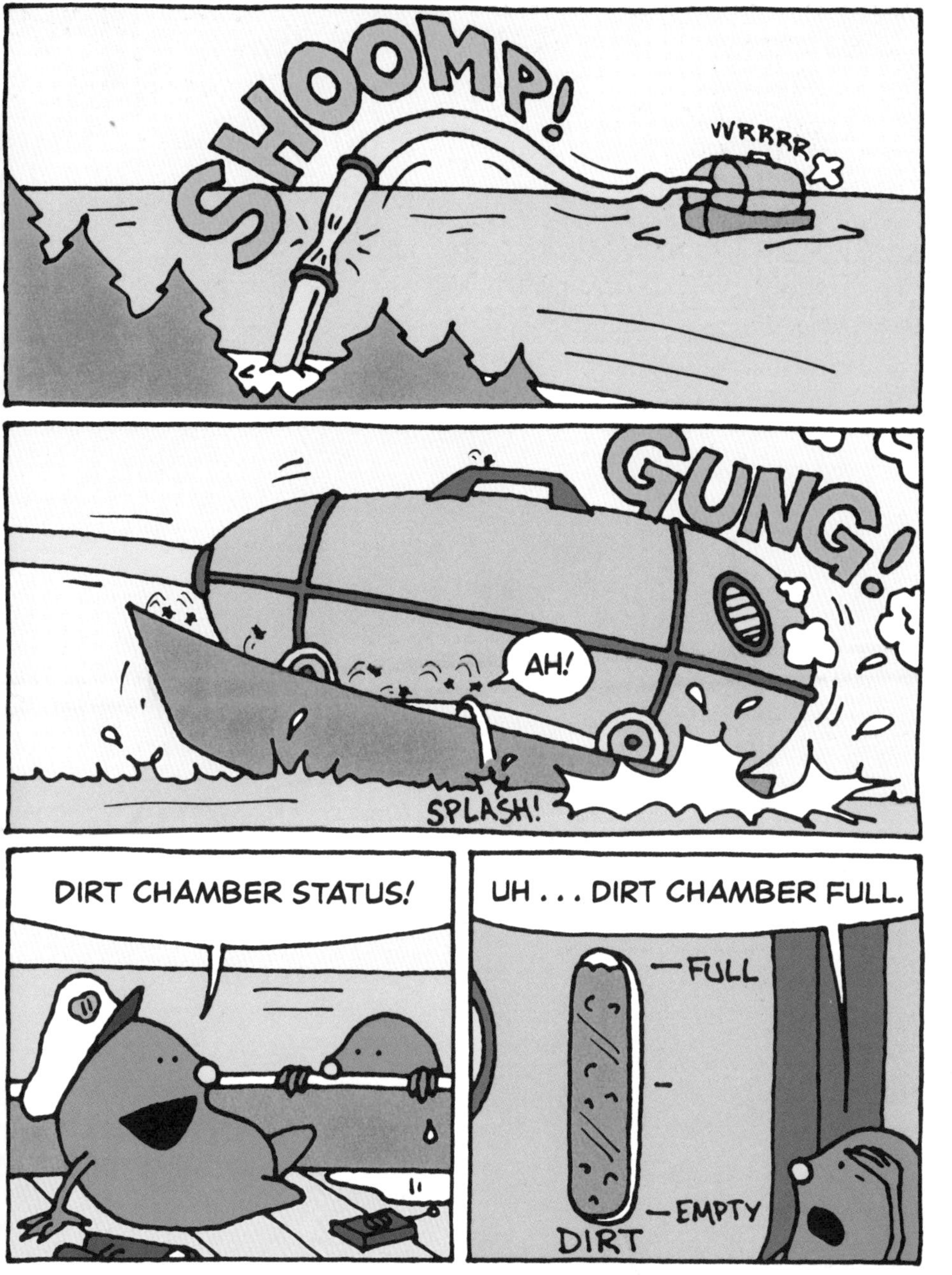
SHOOMP!
VVRRRR
GUNG!
AH!
SPLASH!
DIRT CHAMBER STATUS!
UH . . . DIRT CHAMBER FULL.
FULL
EMPTY
DIRT

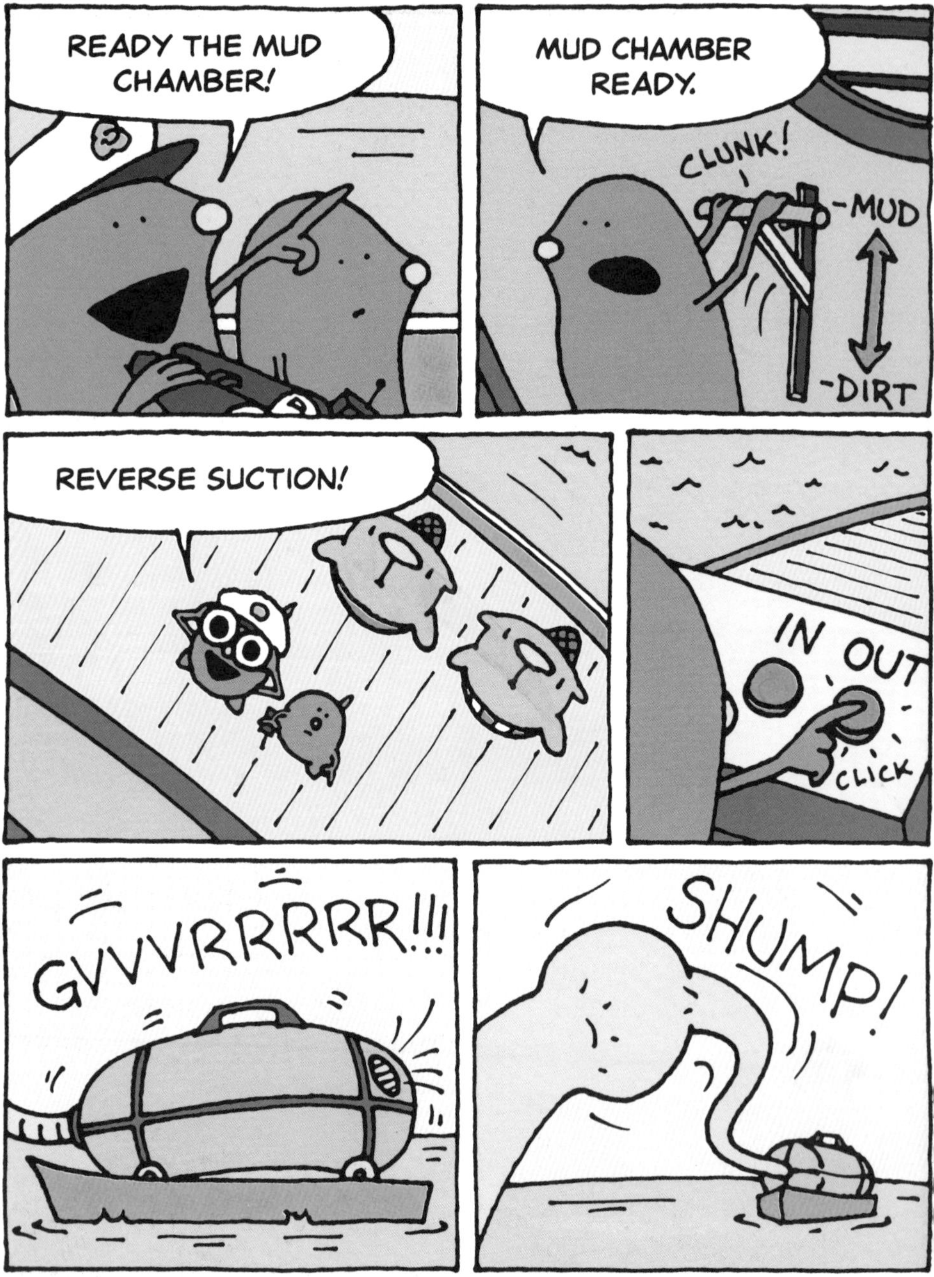
READY THE MUD CHAMBER!
MUD CHAMBER READY.
CLUNK!
-MUD
-DIRT
REVERSE SUCTION!
IN
OUT
CLICK
GVVVRRRRRR!!!
SHUMP!

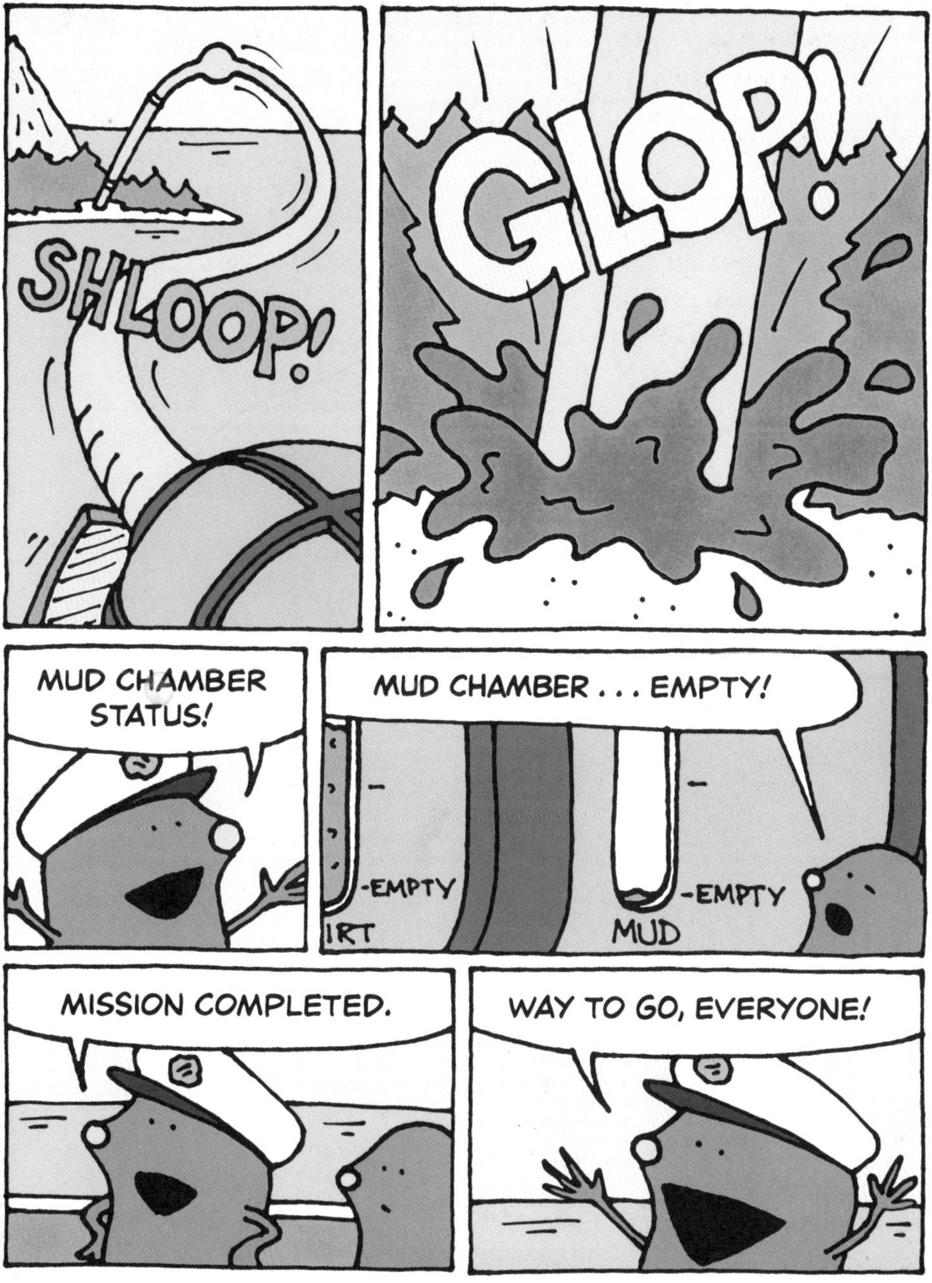
SHLOOP!
GLOP!
MUD CHAMBER STATUS!
MUD CHAMBER . . . EMPTY!
-EMPTY
IRT
-EMPTY
MUD
MISSION COMPLETED.
WAY TO GO, EVERYONE!

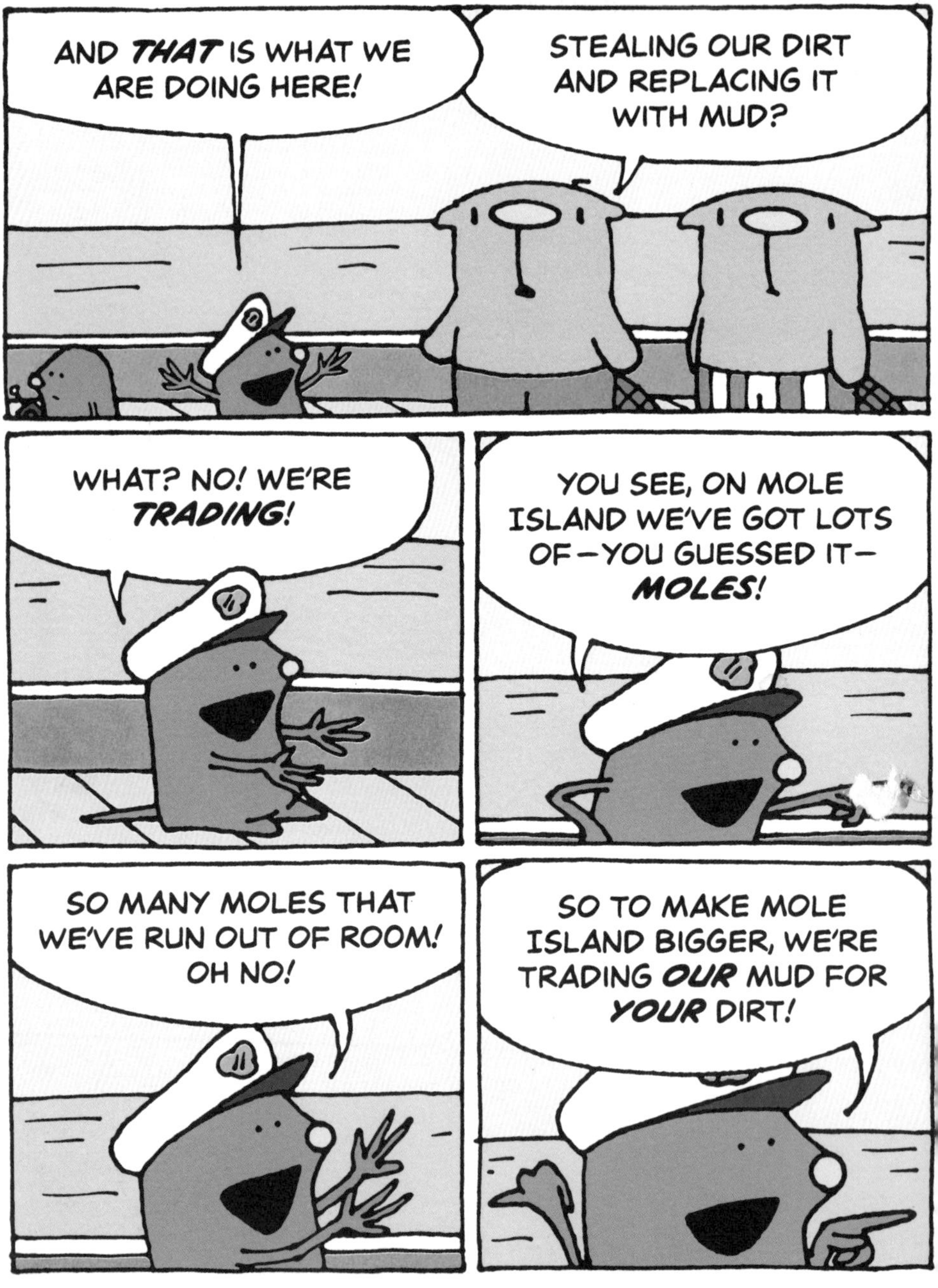
AND *THAT* IS WHAT WE ARE DOING HERE!
STEALING OUR DIRT AND REPLACING IT WITH MUD?
WHAT? NO! WE'RE *TRADING*!
YOU SEE, ON MOLE ISLAND WE'VE GOT LOTS OF—YOU GUESSED IT—*MOLES*!
SO MANY MOLES THAT WE'VE RUN OUT OF ROOM! OH NO!
SO TO MAKE MOLE ISLAND BIGGER, WE'RE TRADING *OUR* MUD FOR *YOUR* DIRT!

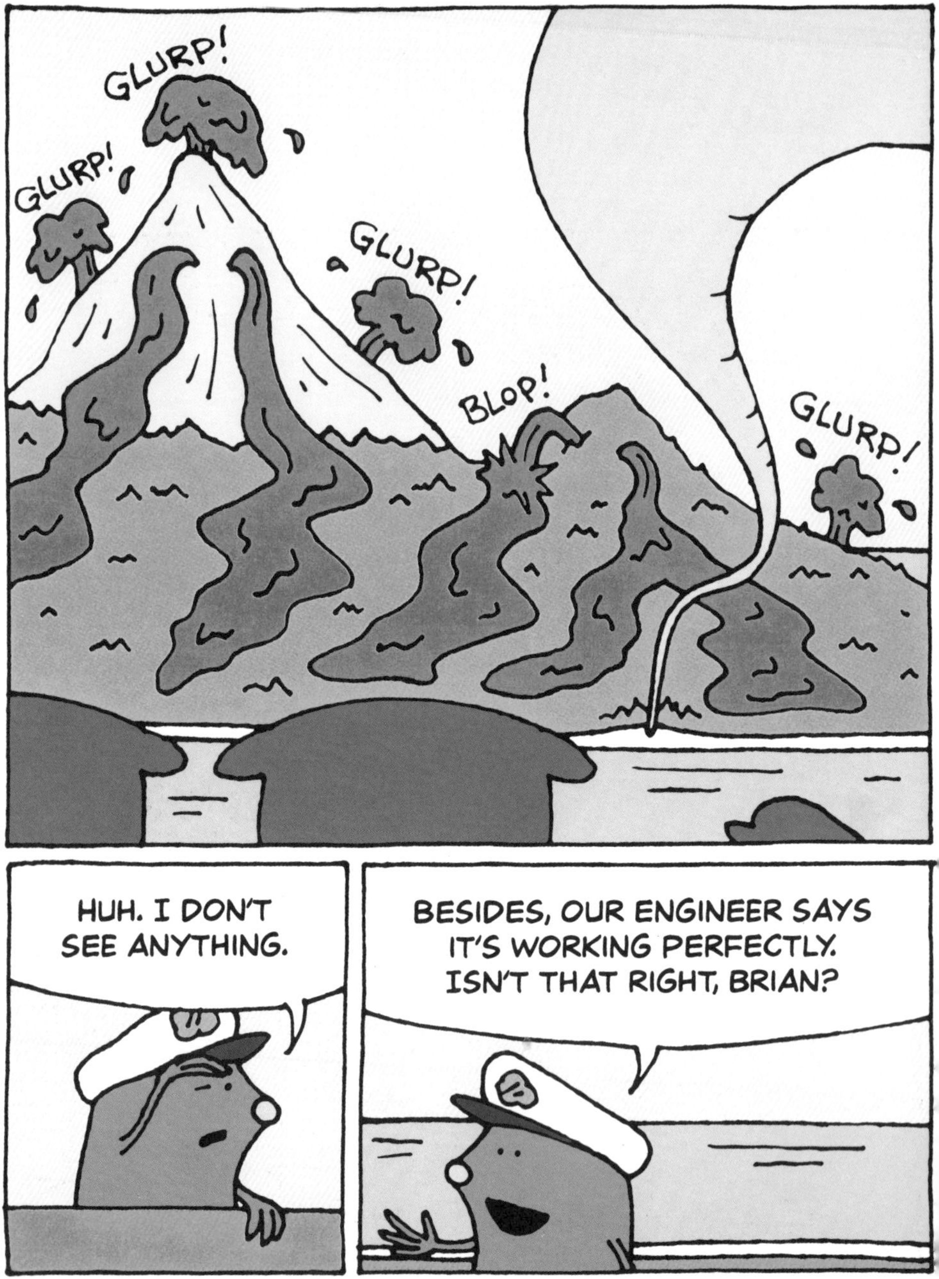
GLURP!
GLURP!
GLURP!
BLOP!
GLURP!
HUH. I DON'T SEE ANYTHING.
BESIDES, OUR ENGINEER SAYS IT'S WORKING PERFECTLY. ISN'T THAT RIGHT, BRIAN?

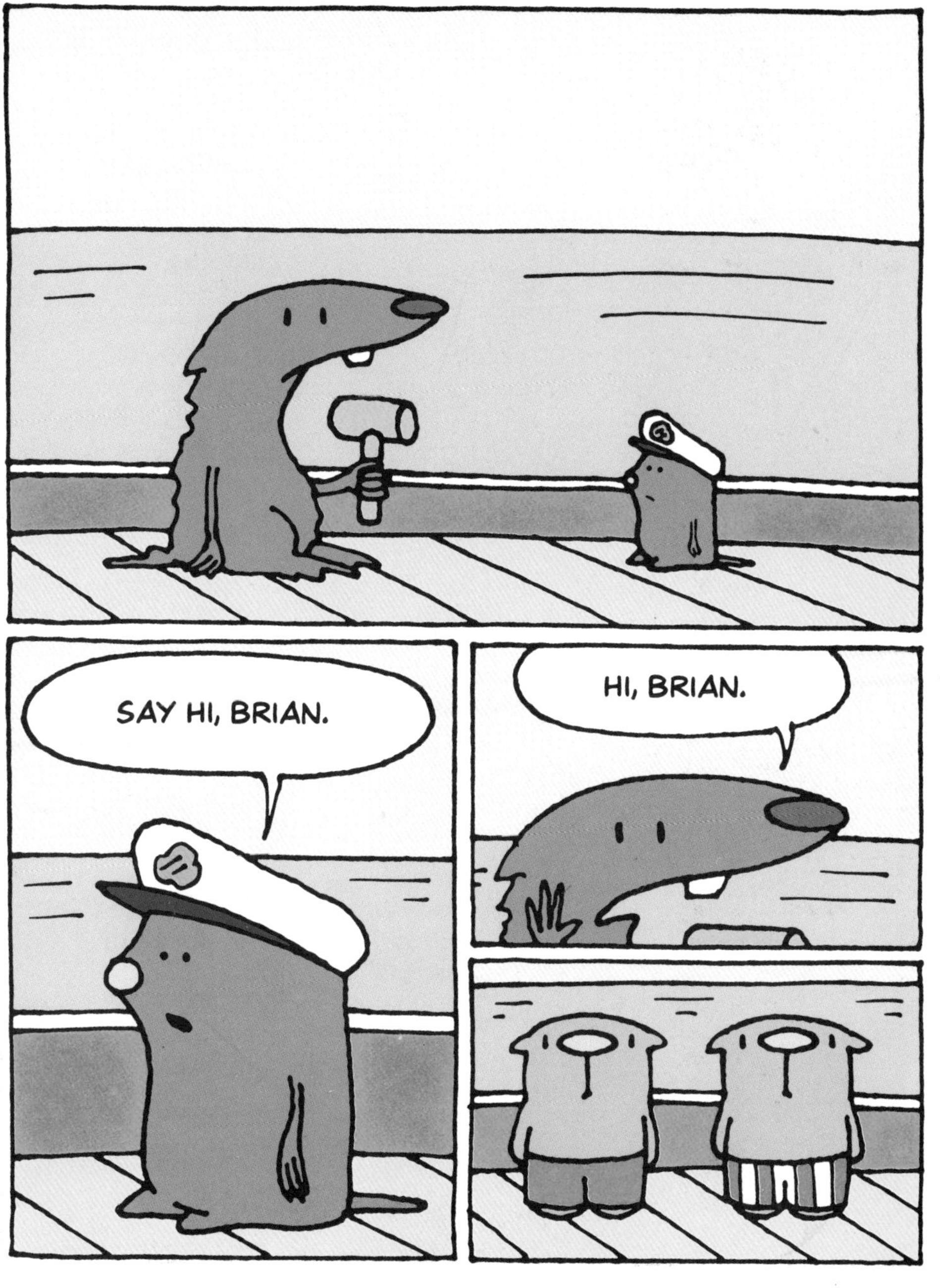
SAY HI, BRIAN.
HI, BRIAN.

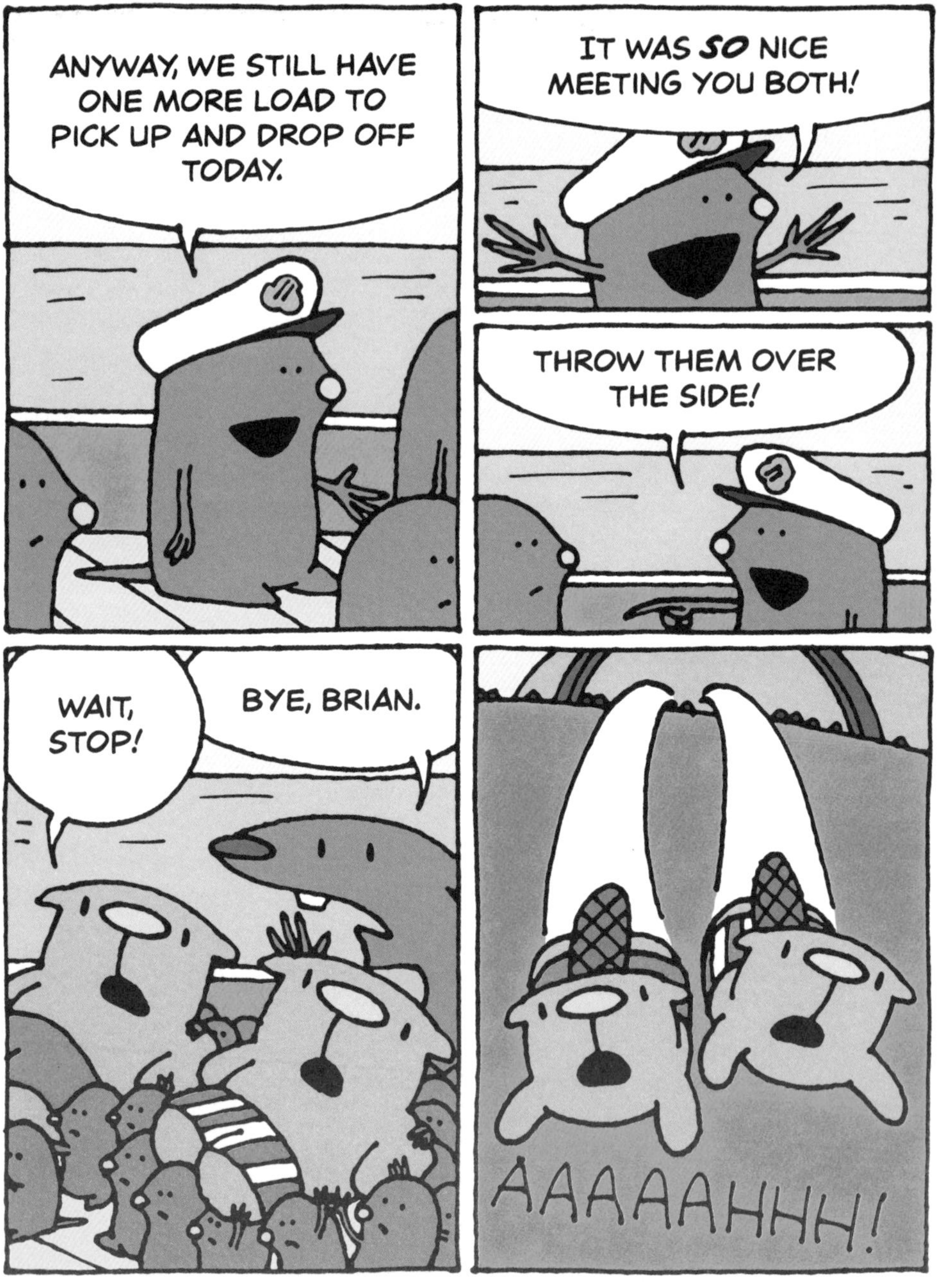
ANYWAY, WE STILL HAVE ONE MORE LOAD TO PICK UP AND DROP OFF TODAY.
IT WAS SO NICE MEETING YOU BOTH!
THROW THEM OVER THE SIDE!
WAIT, STOP!
BYE, BRIAN.
AAAAAHHH!

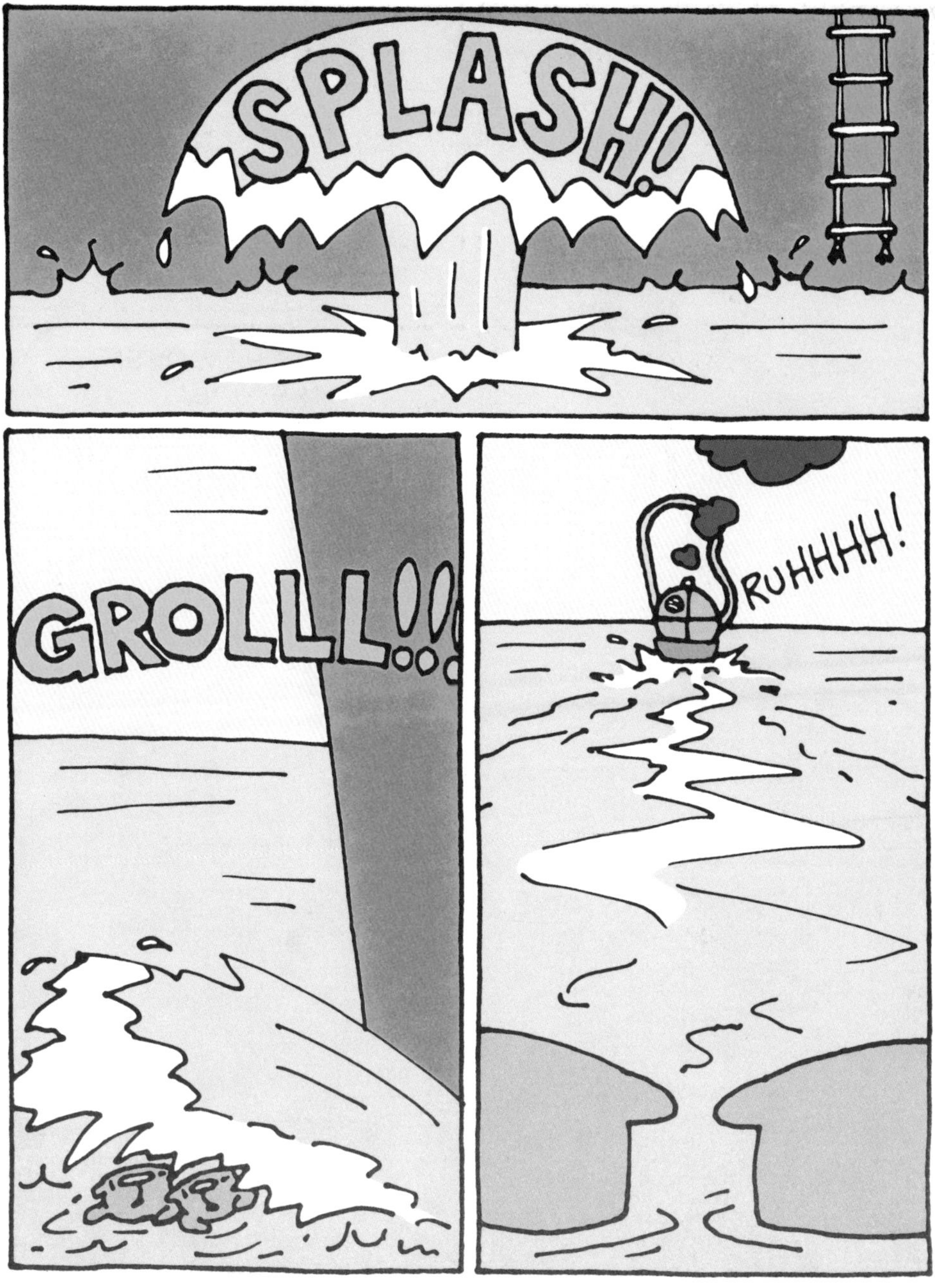
SPLASH!
GROLLL!!!
RUHHHH!

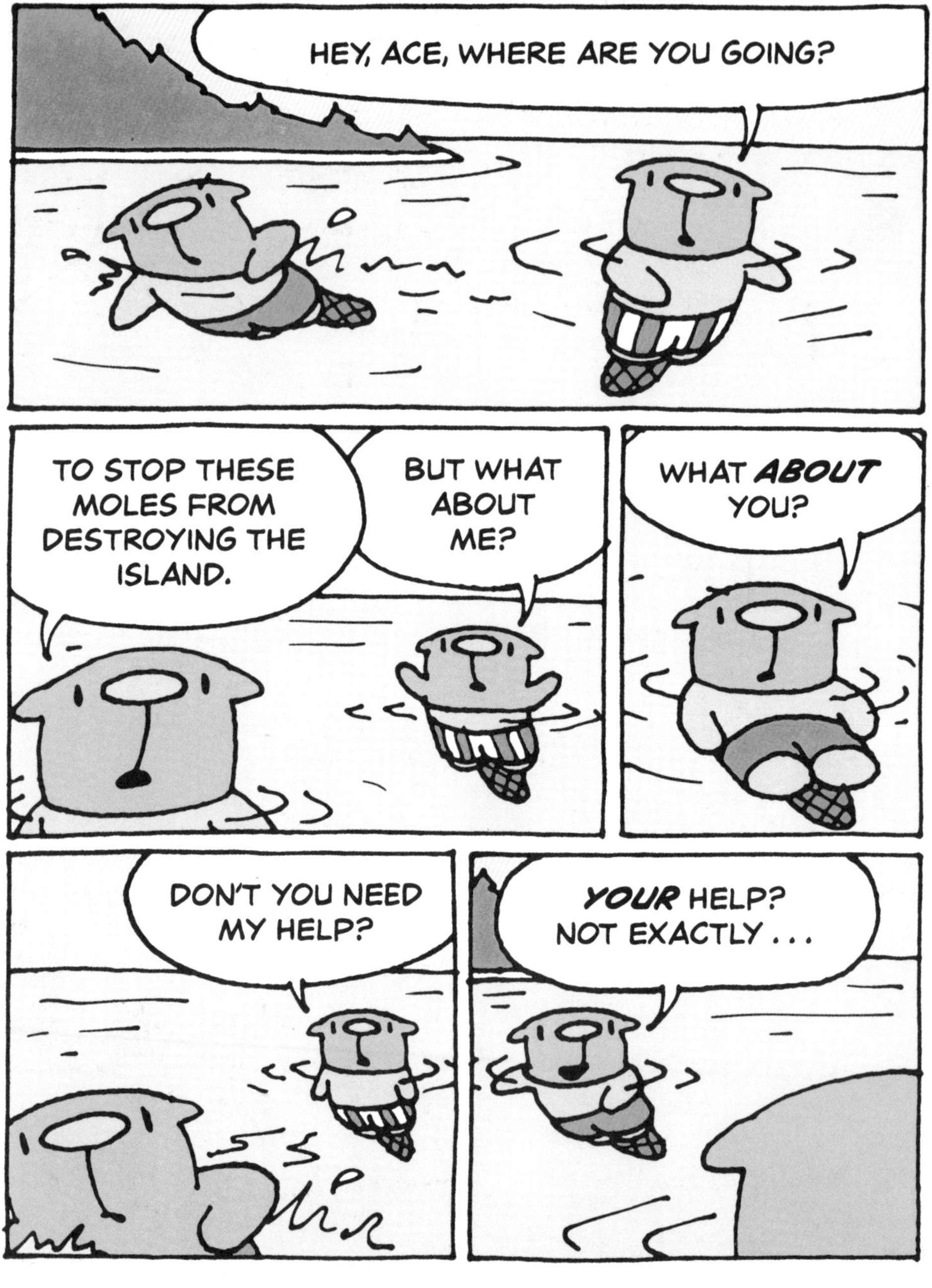
HEY, ACE, WHERE ARE YOU GOING?
TO STOP THESE MOLES FROM DESTROYING THE ISLAND.
BUT WHAT ABOUT ME?
WHAT *ABOUT* YOU?
DON'T YOU NEED MY HELP?
YOUR HELP? NOT EXACTLY . . .

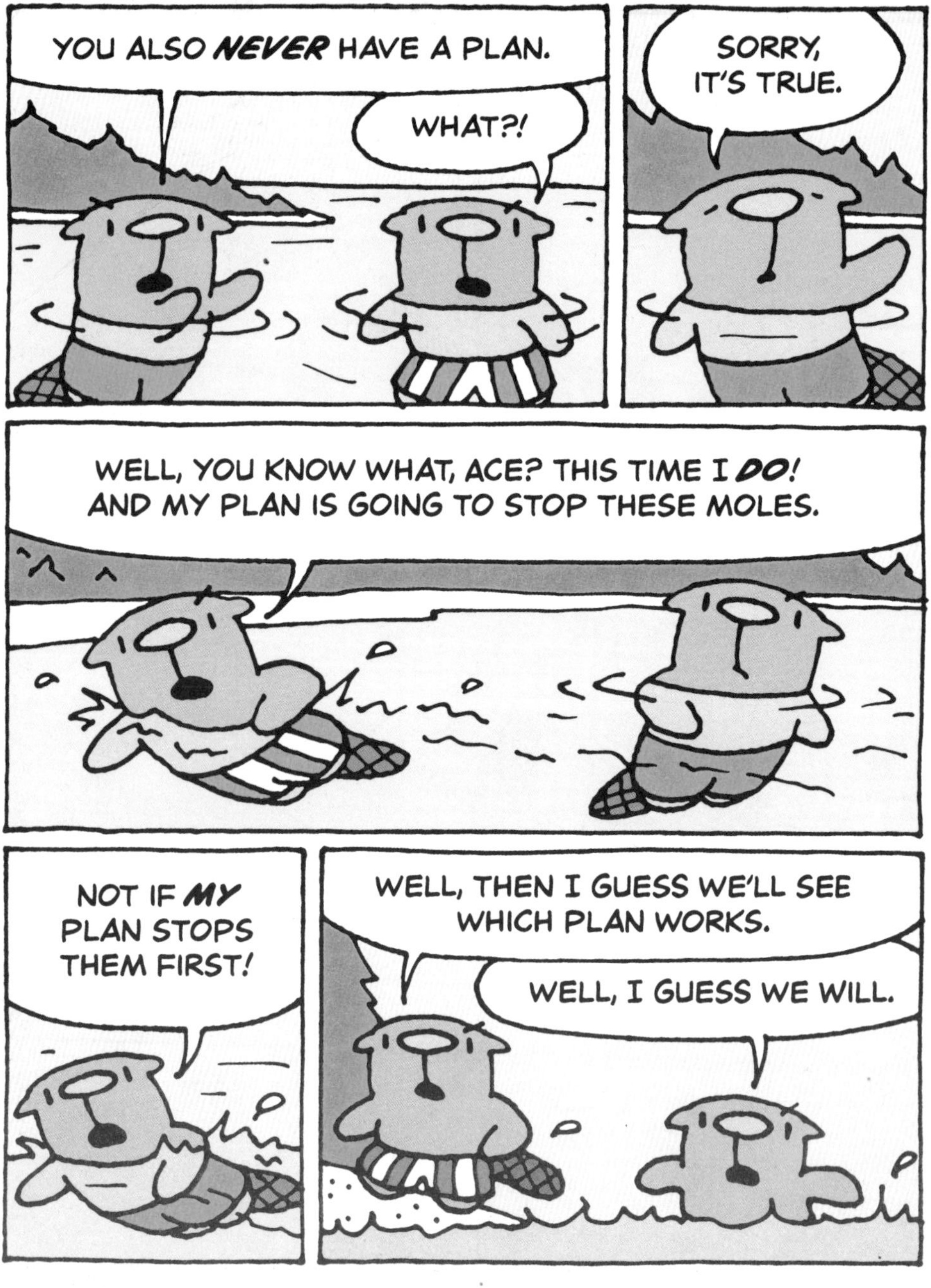
YOU ALSO NEVER HAVE A PLAN.
WHAT?!
SORRY, IT'S TRUE.
WELL, YOU KNOW WHAT, ACE? THIS TIME I DO! AND MY PLAN IS GOING TO STOP THESE MOLES.
NOT IF MY PLAN STOPS THEM FIRST!
WELL, THEN I GUESS WE'LL SEE WHICH PLAN WORKS.
WELL, I GUESS WE WILL.

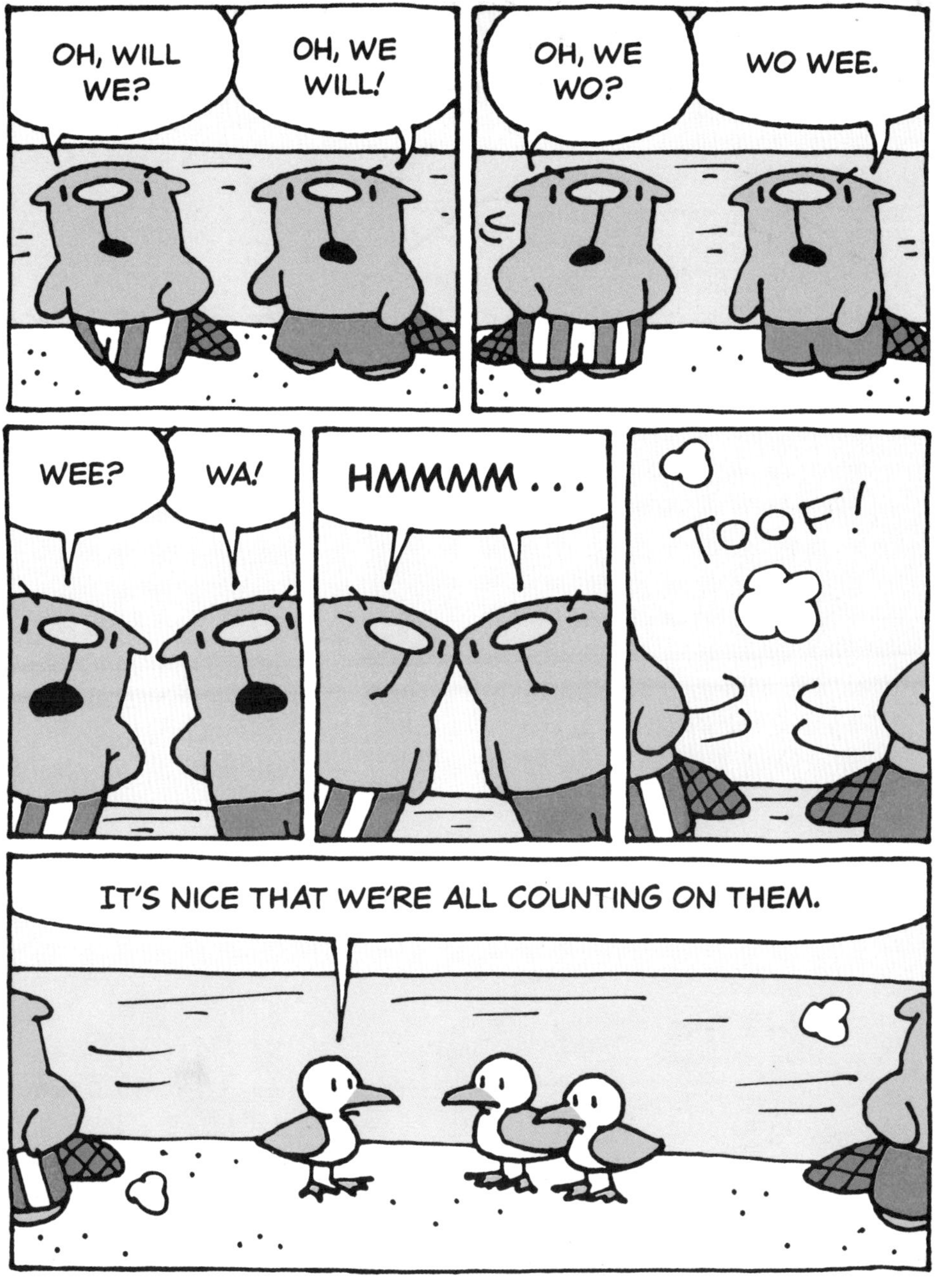

OH, WILL WE?
OH, WE WILL!
OH, WE WO?
WO WEE.
WEE?
WA!
HMMMM . . .
TOOF!
IT'S NICE THAT WE'RE ALL COUNTING ON THEM.

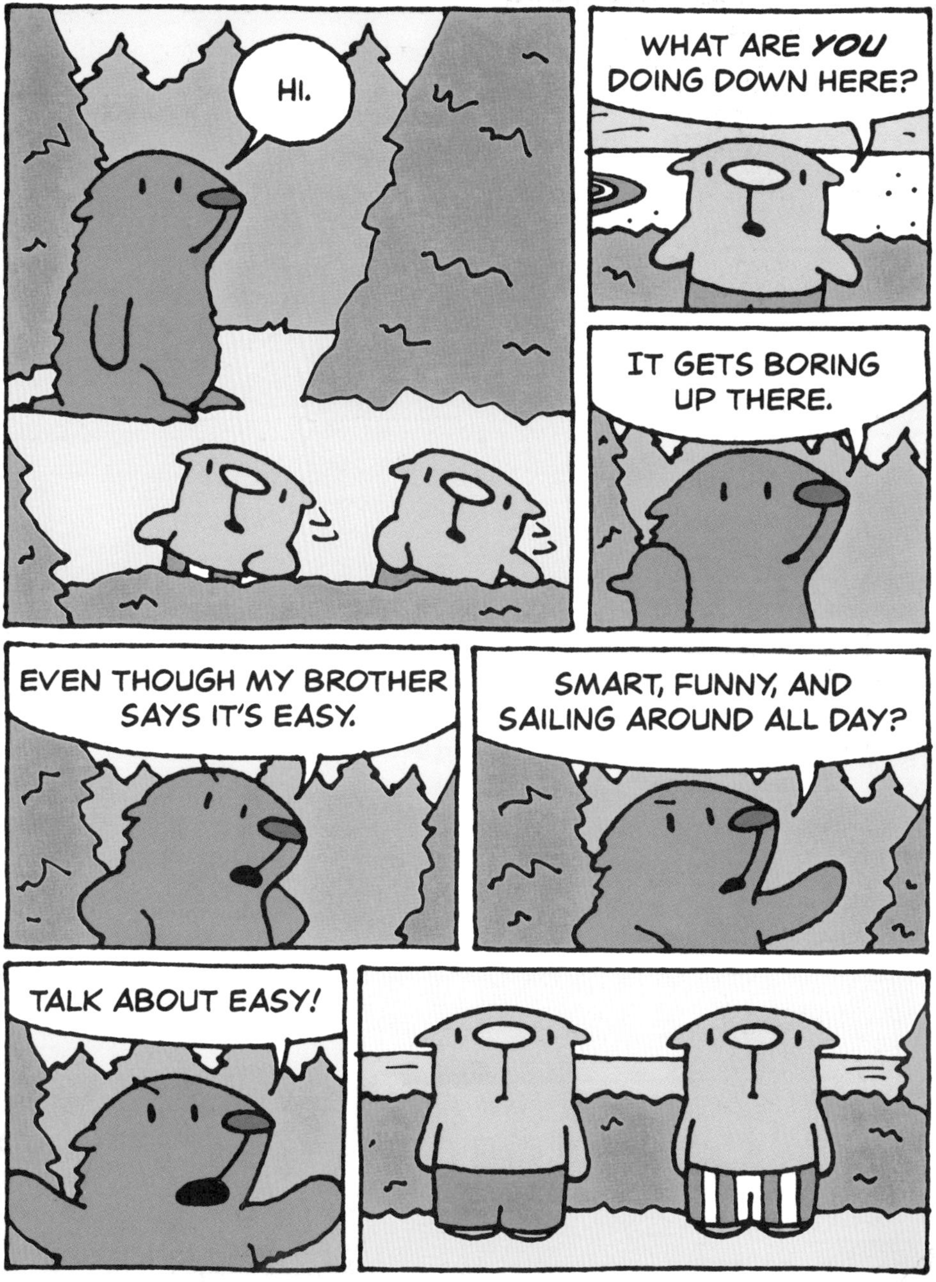
HI.
WHAT ARE *YOU* DOING DOWN HERE?
IT GETS BORING UP THERE.
EVEN THOUGH MY BROTHER SAYS IT'S EASY.
SMART, FUNNY, AND SAILING AROUND ALL DAY?
TALK ABOUT EASY!

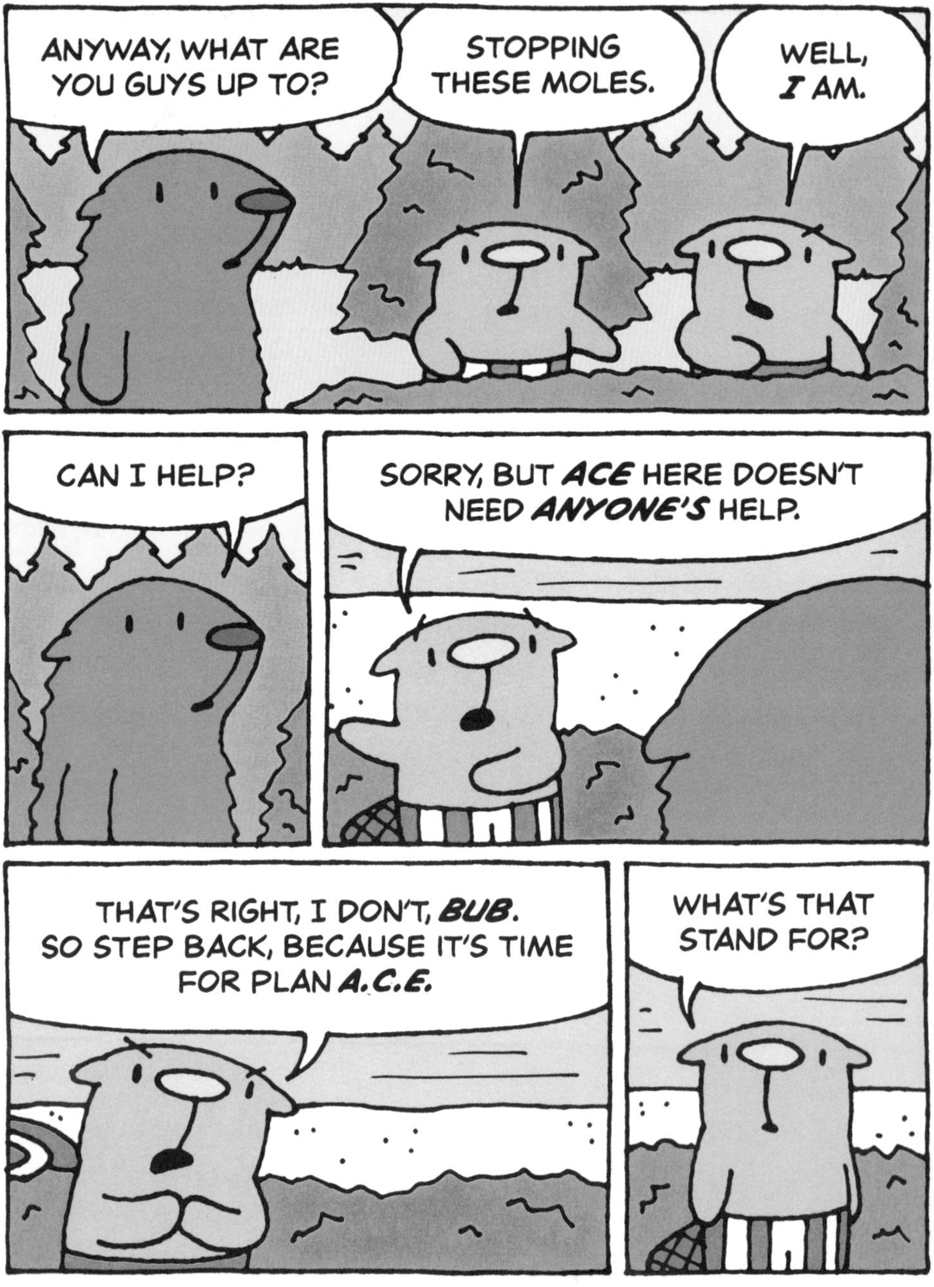
ANYWAY, WHAT ARE YOU GUYS UP TO?
STOPPING THESE MOLES.
WELL, *I* AM.
CAN I HELP?
SORRY, BUT *ACE* HERE DOESN'T NEED *ANYONE'S* HELP.
THAT'S RIGHT, I DON'T, *BUB*. SO STEP BACK, BECAUSE IT'S TIME FOR PLAN *A.C.E.*
WHAT'S THAT STAND FOR?

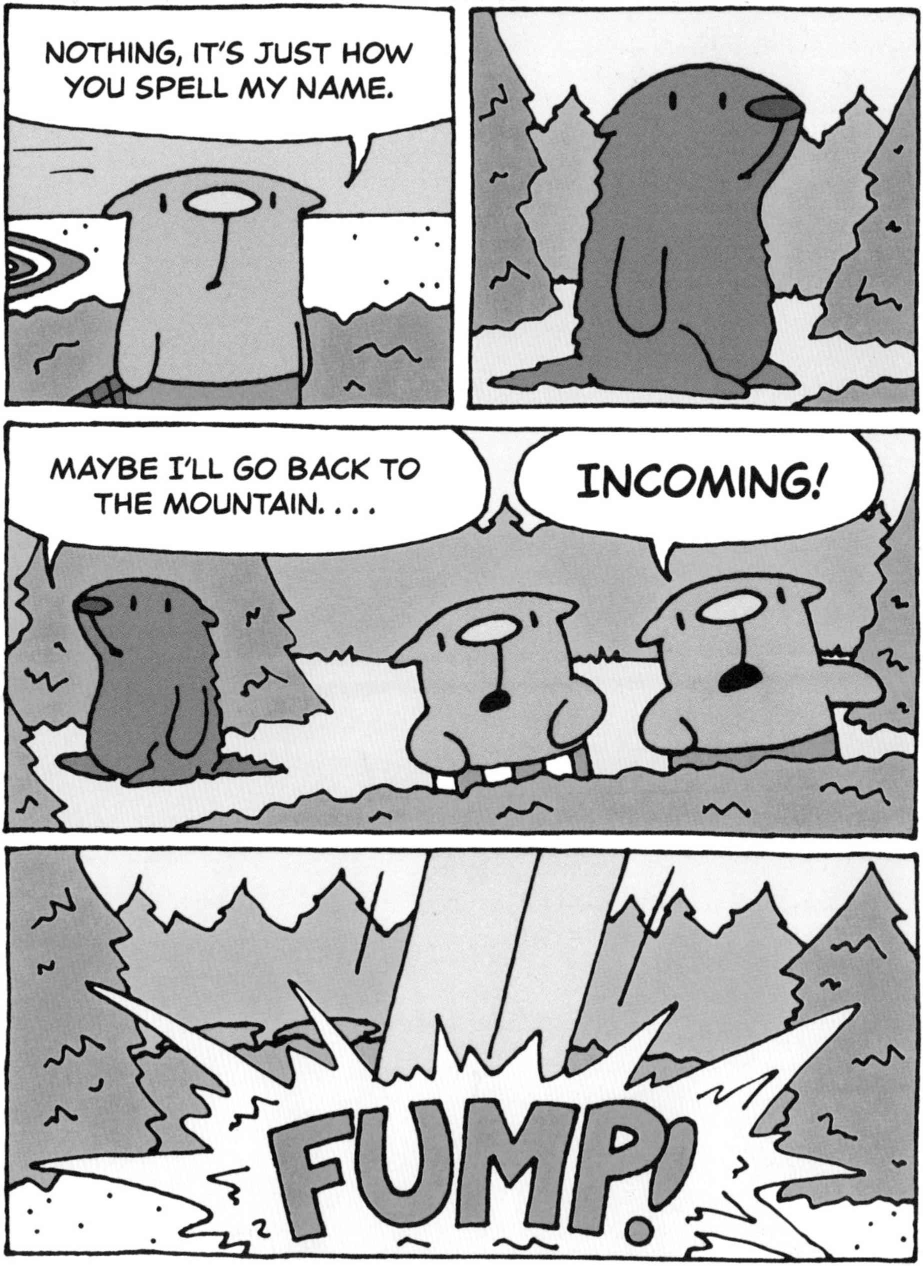
NOTHING, IT'S JUST HOW YOU SPELL MY NAME.
MAYBE I'LL GO BACK TO THE MOUNTAIN. . . .
INCOMING!
FUMP!

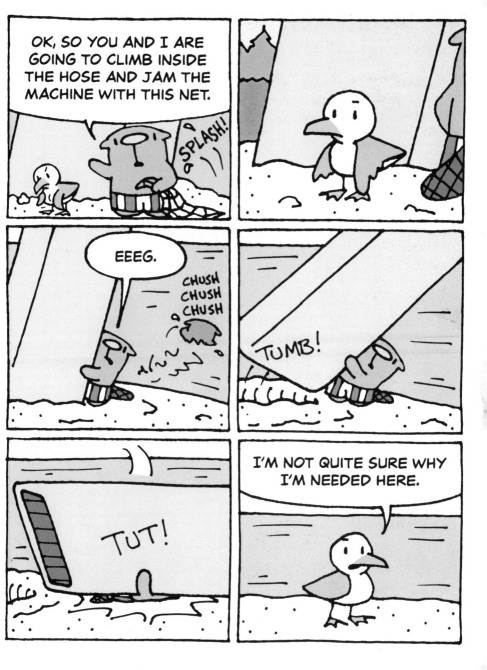

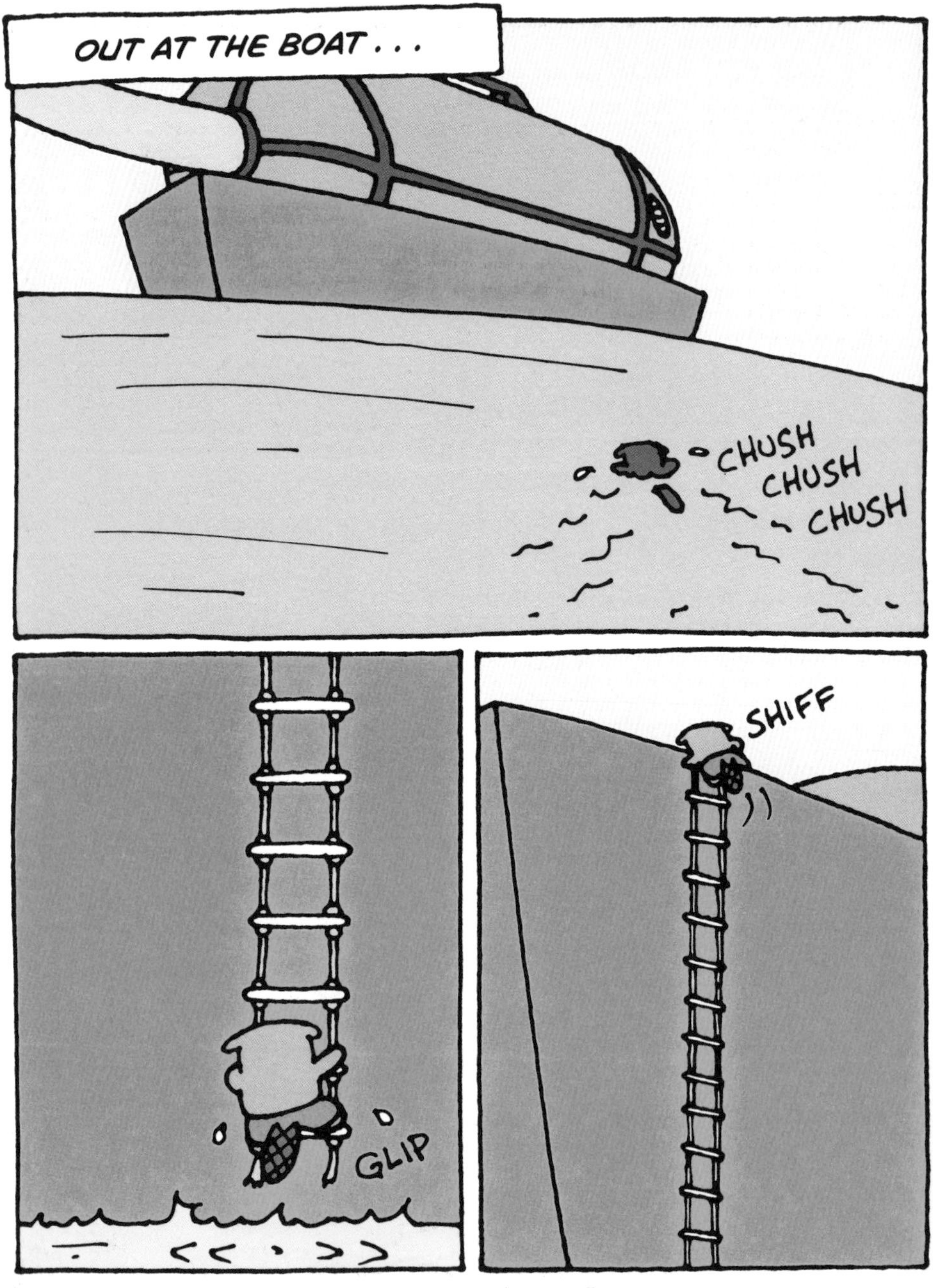
OUT AT THE BOAT . . .
CHUSH
CHUSH
CHUSH
GLIP
SHIFF

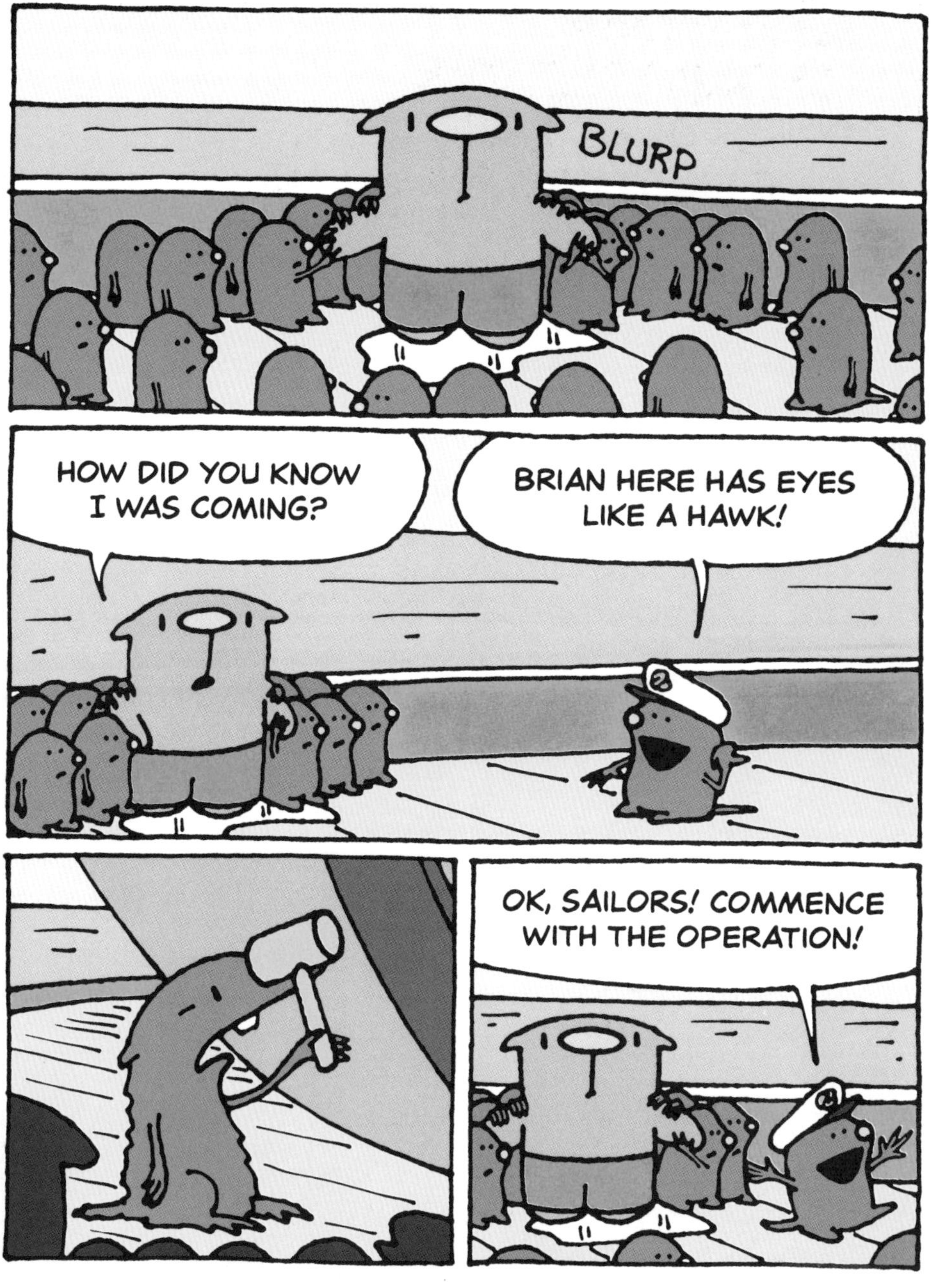
BLURP
HOW DID YOU KNOW I WAS COMING?
BRIAN HERE HAS EYES LIKE A HAWK!
OK, SAILORS! COMMENCE WITH THE OPERATION!

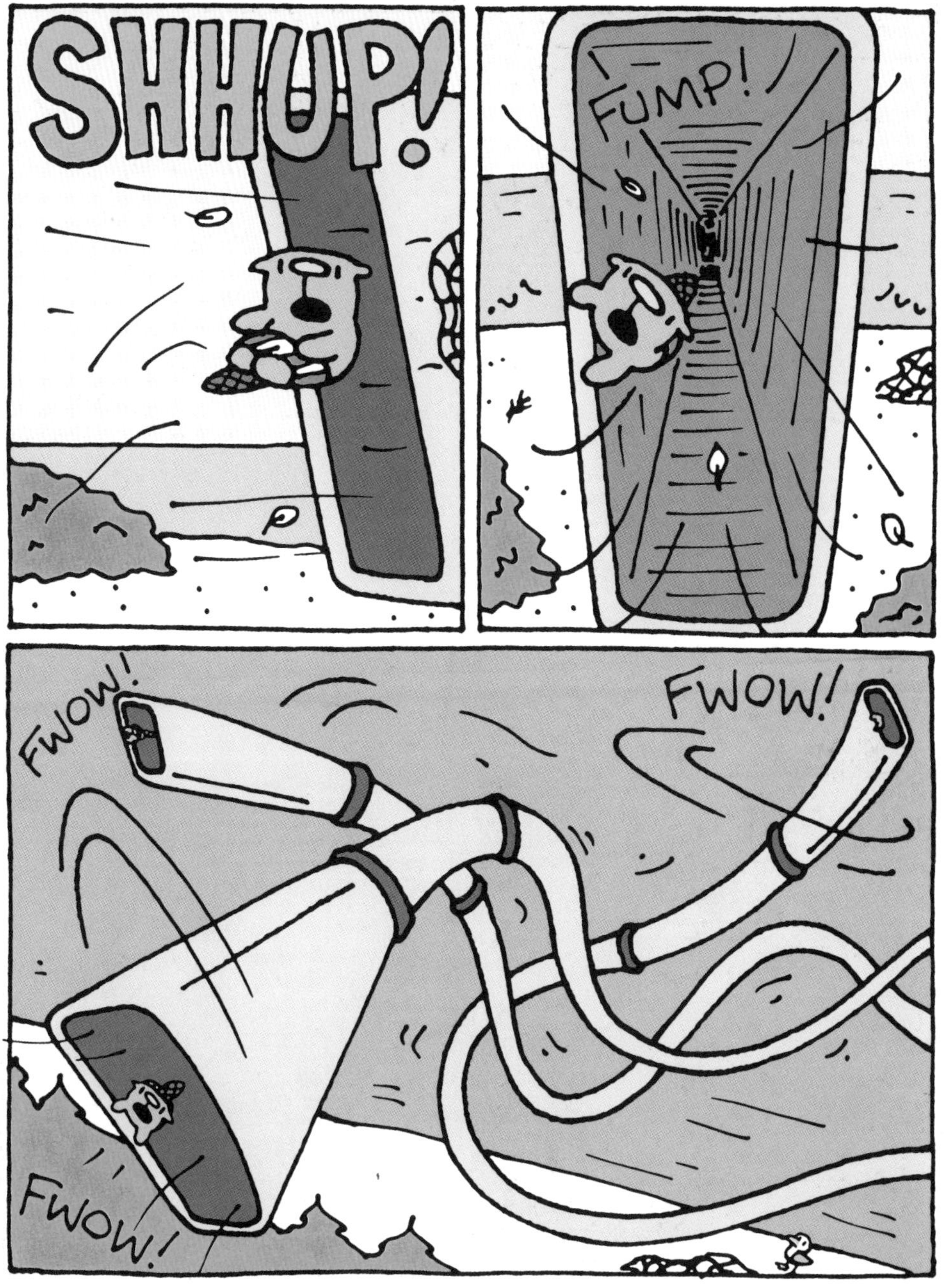
SHHUP!
FUMP!
FWOW!
FWOW!
FWOW!

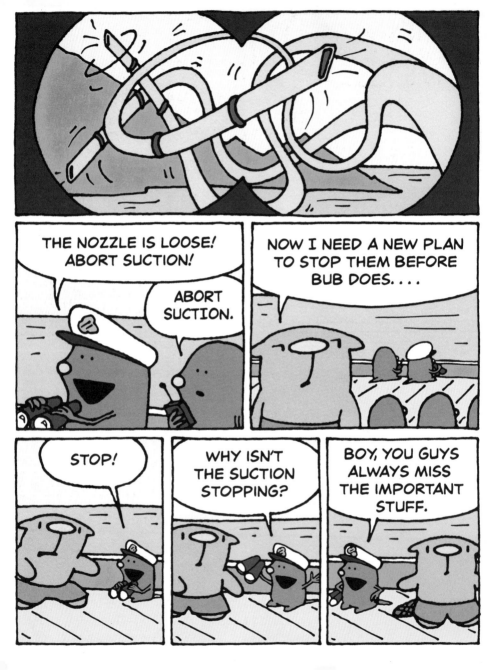

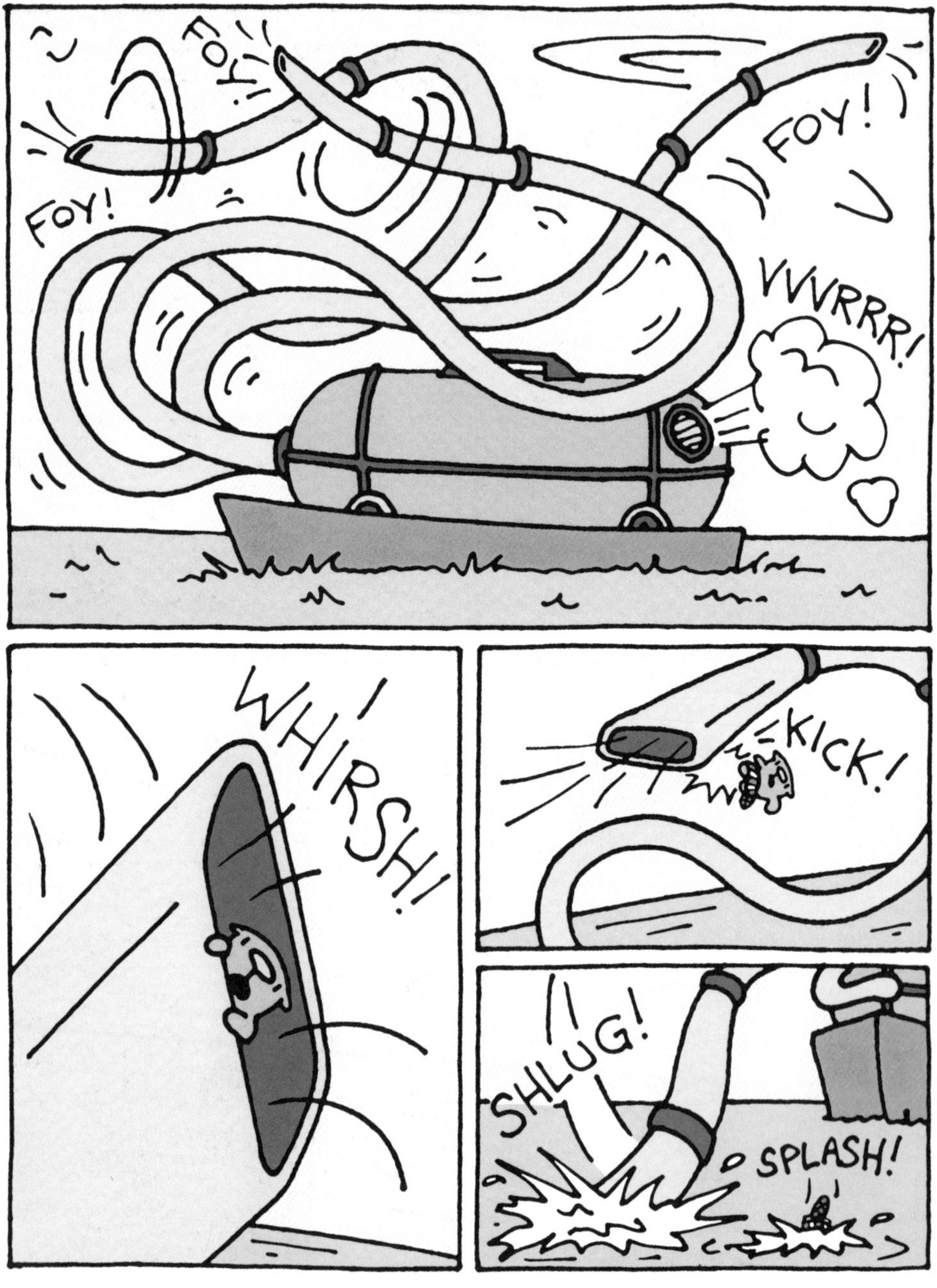
FOY!
FOY!
FOY!
VVVRRRR!
WHIRSH!
KICK!
SHLUG!
SPLASH!

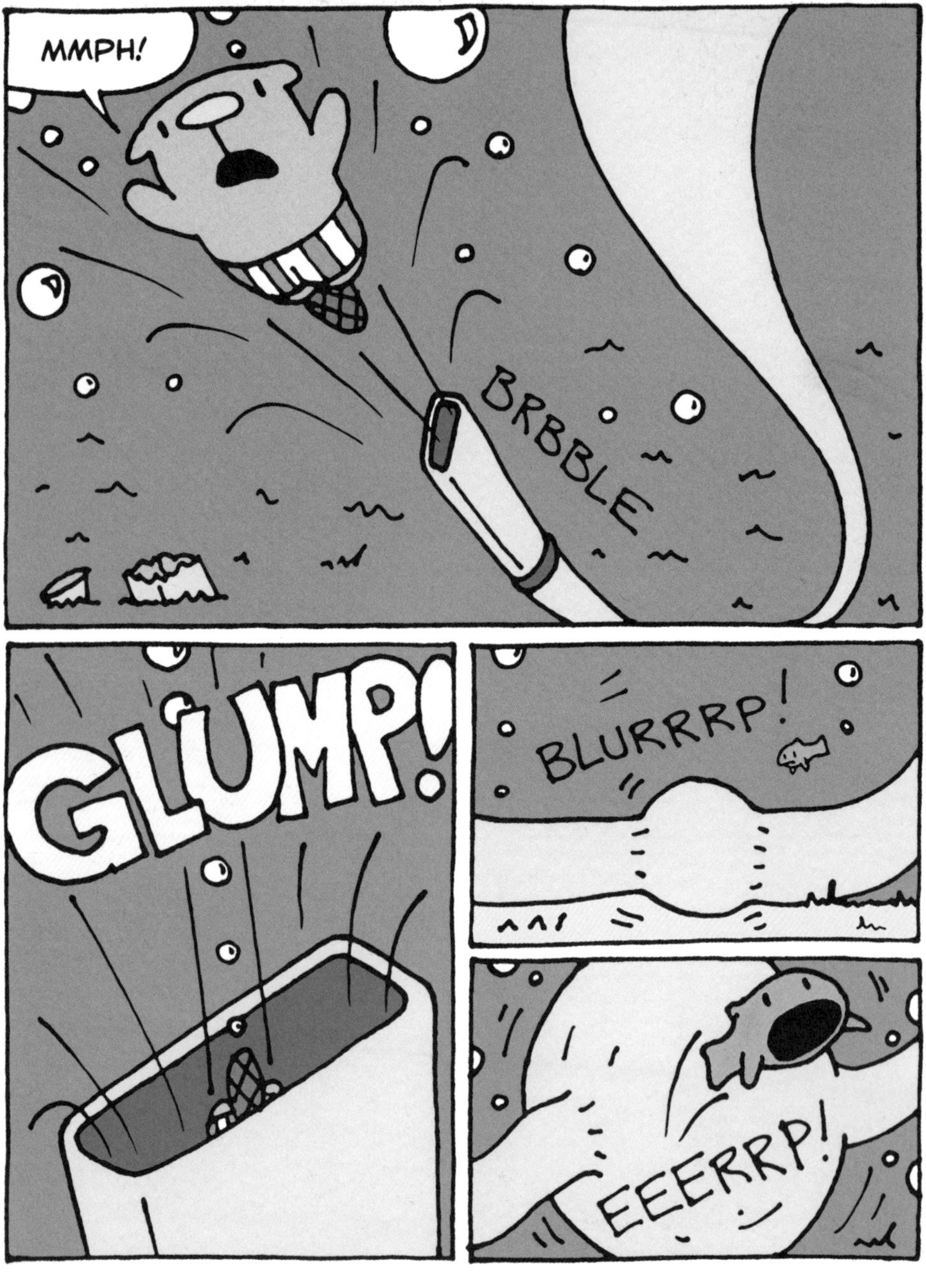
MMPH!
BRBBLE
GLUMP!
BLURRRP!
EEERRP!

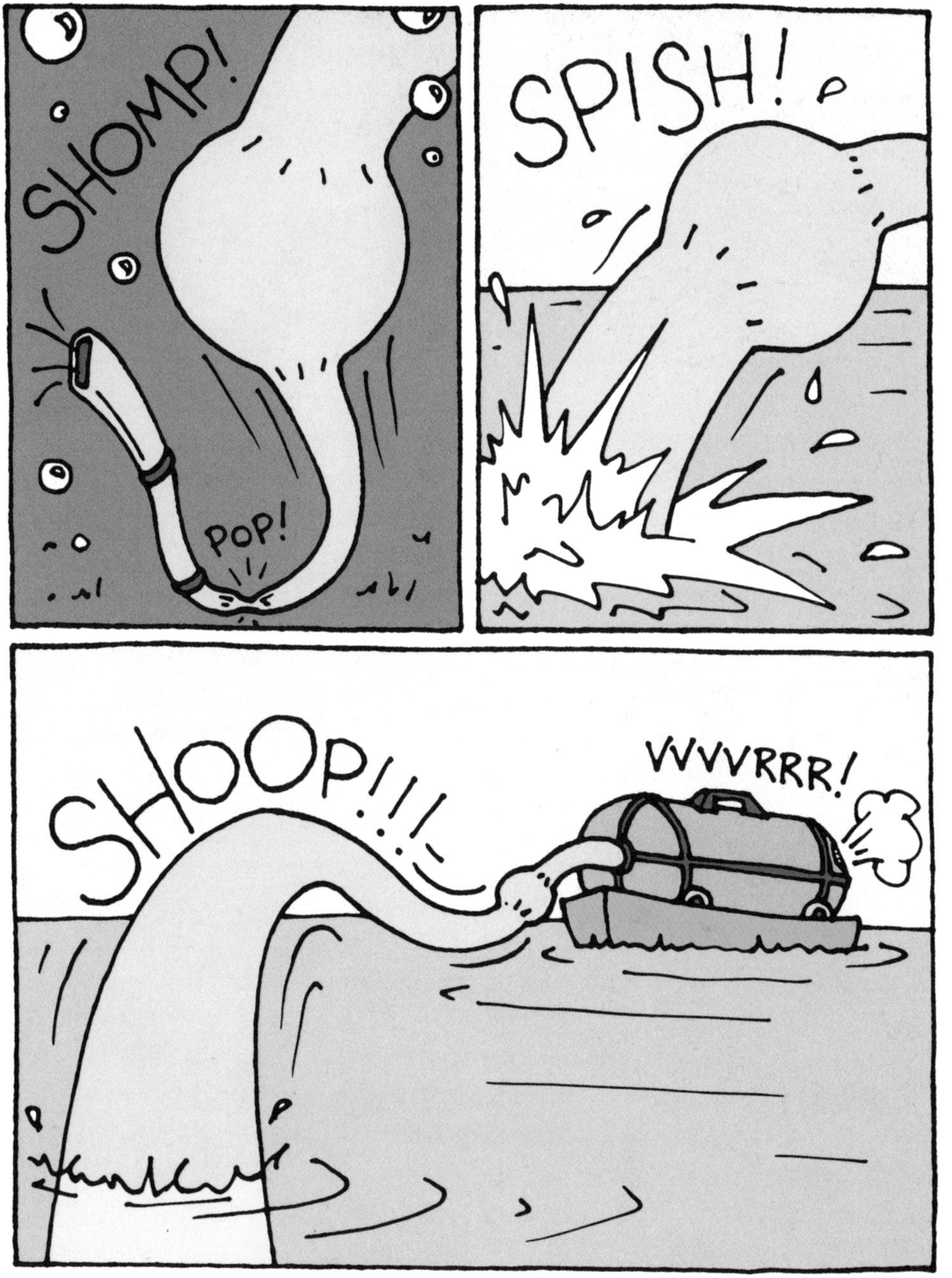
SHOMP!
POP!
SPISH!
SHOOP!!!
VVVVRRR!

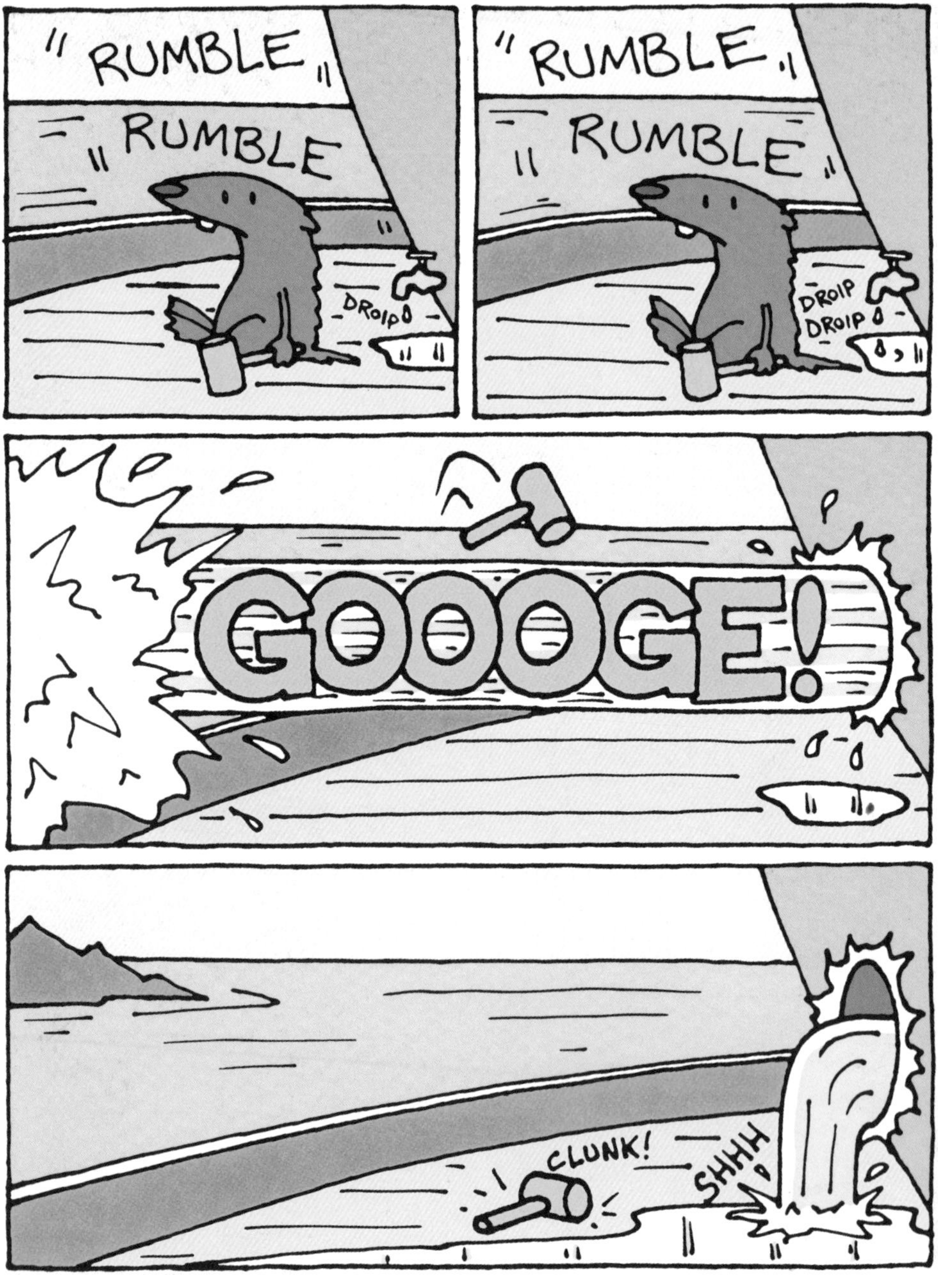
"RUMBLE"
"RUMBLE"
DROIP
"RUMBLE"
"RUMBLE"
DROIP
DROIP
GOOOGE!
CLUNK!
SHHH

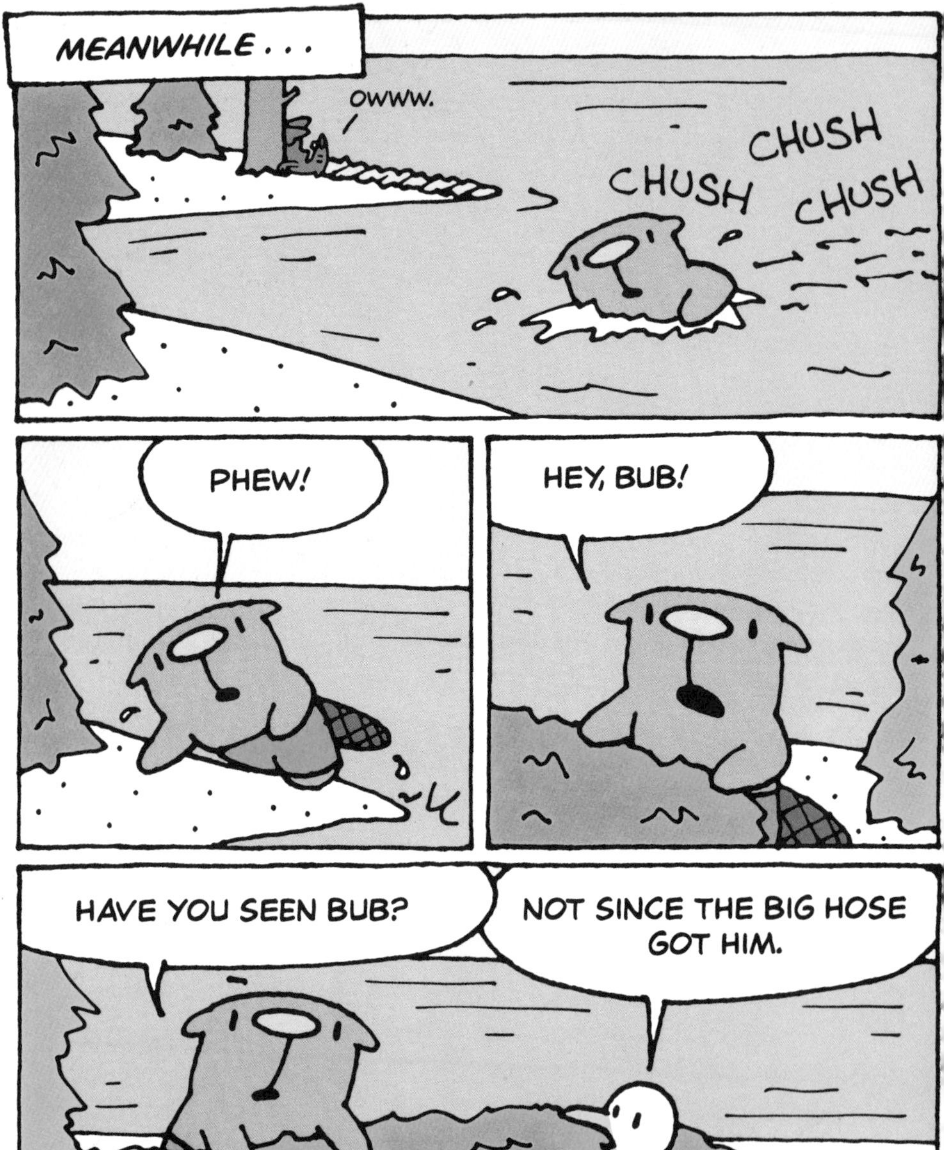
MEANWHILE . . .
OWWW.
CHUSH
CHUSH
CHUSH
PHEW!
HEY, BUB!
HAVE YOU SEEN BUB?
NOT SINCE THE BIG HOSE GOT HIM.

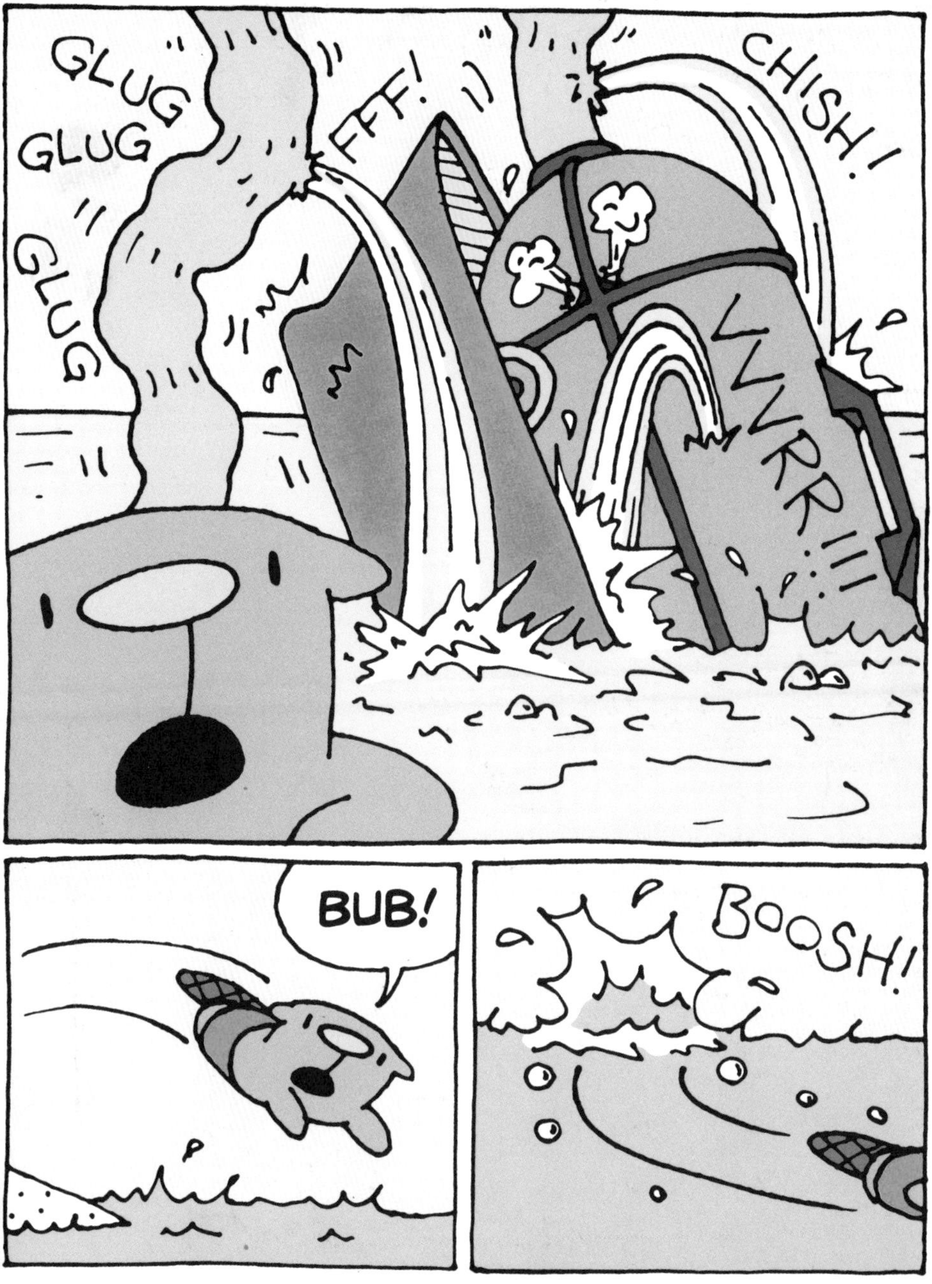
GLUG
GLUG
GLUG
FFF!
CHISH!
VVVRR
BUB!
BOOSH!

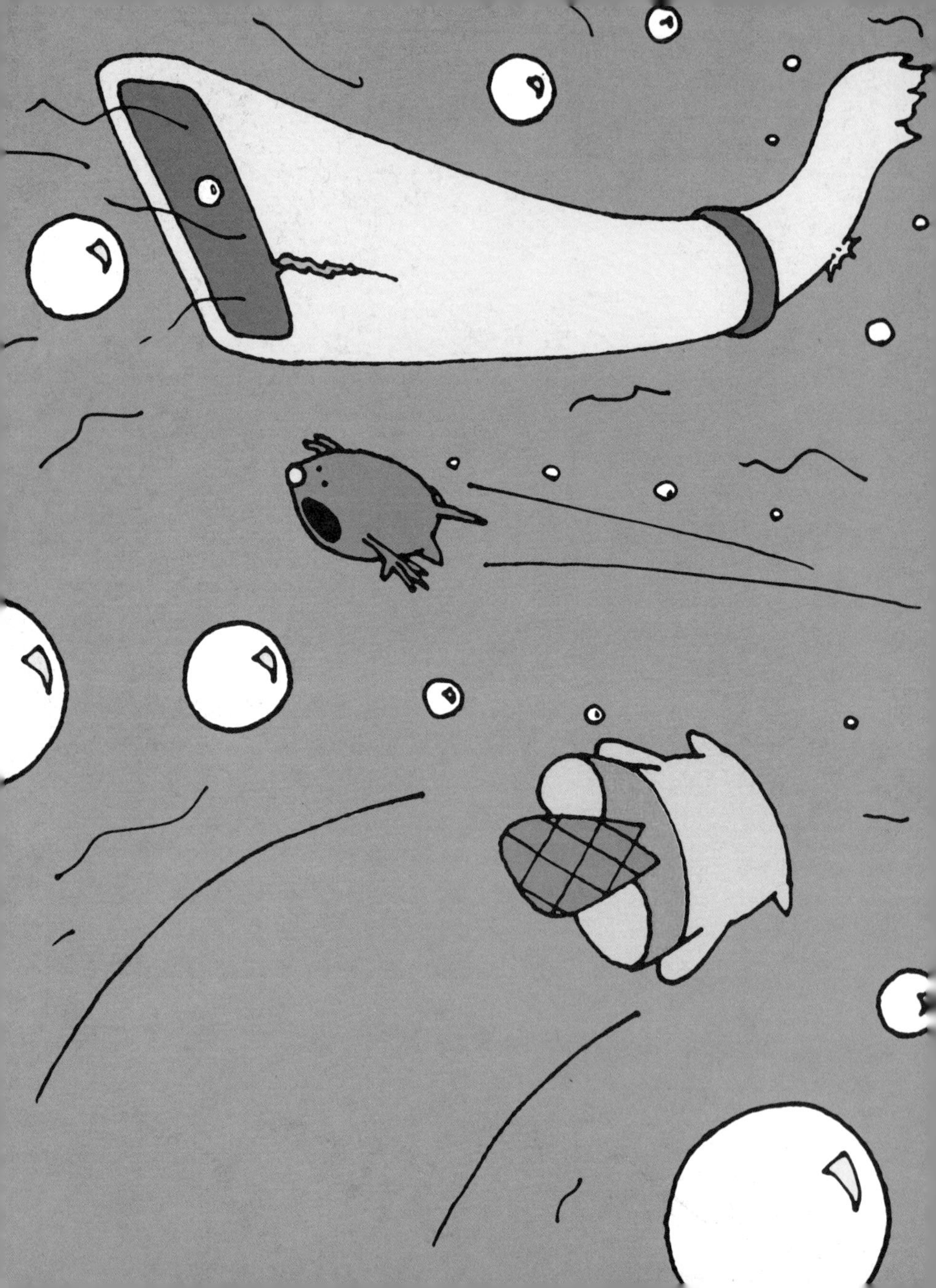

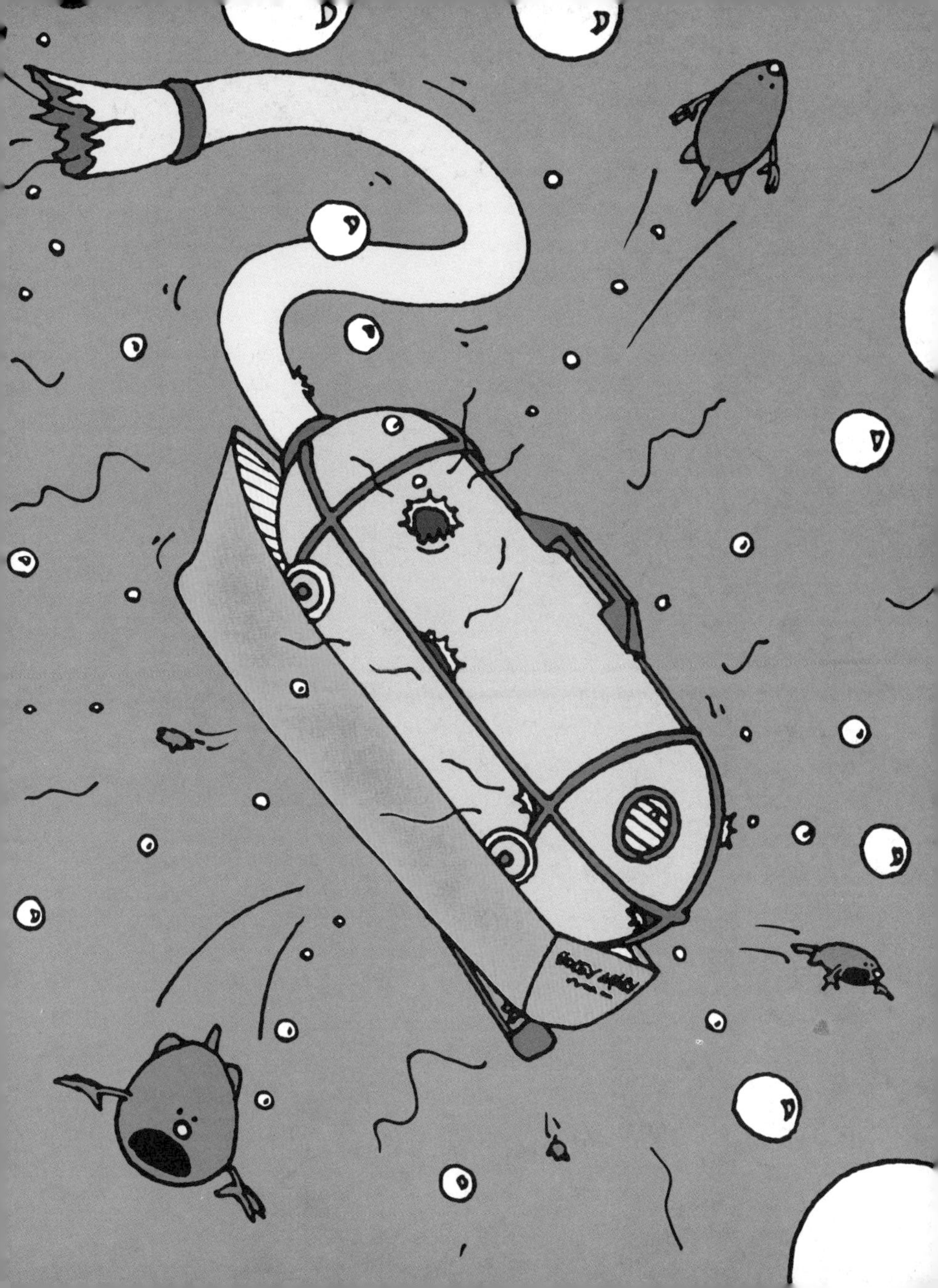

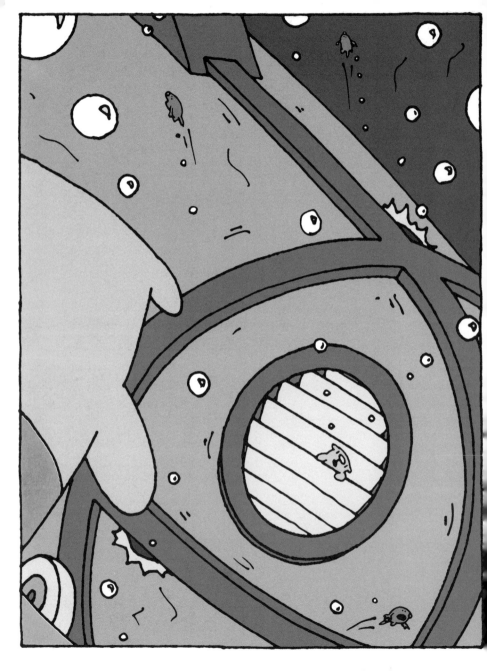

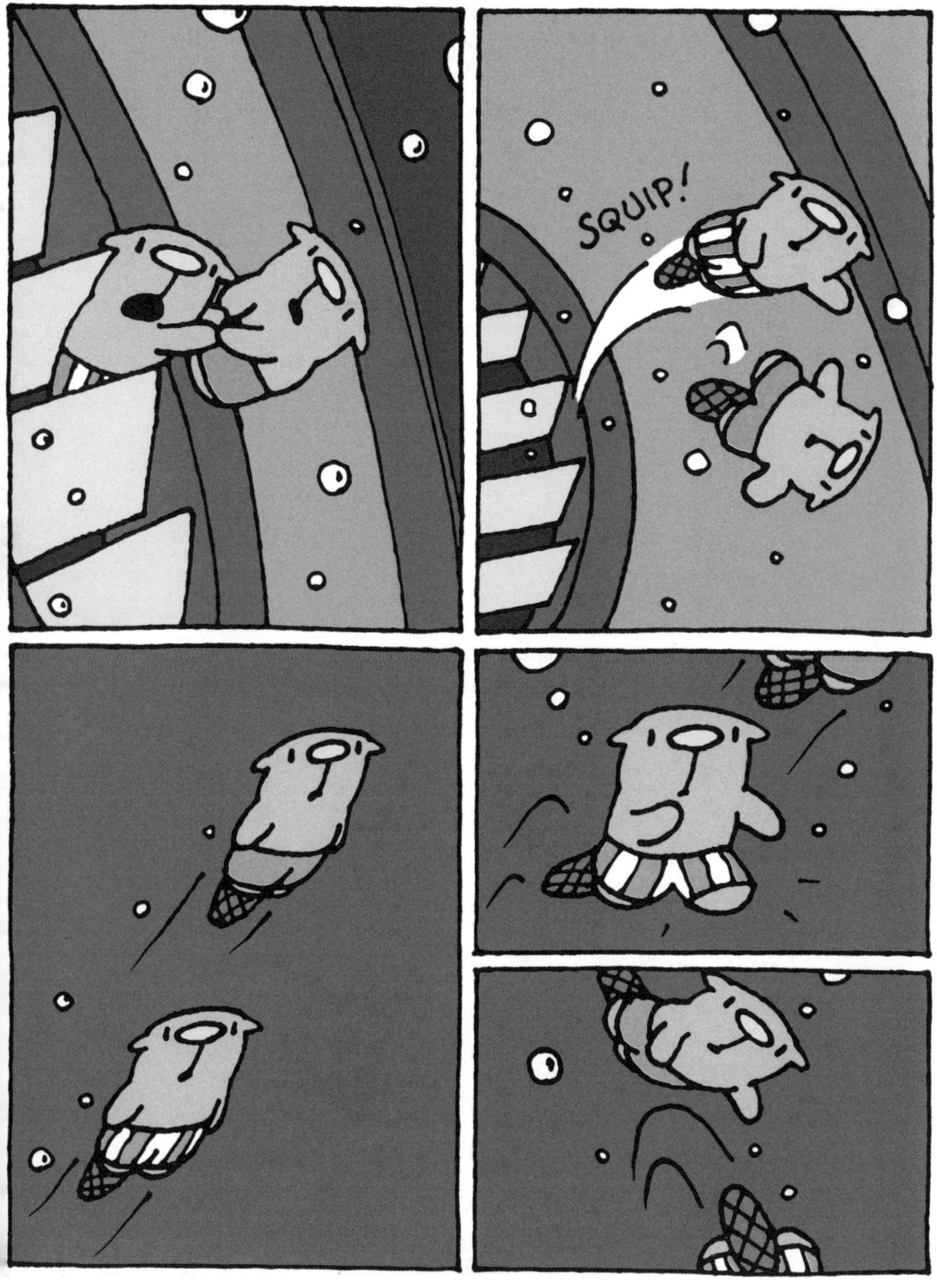
SQUIP!

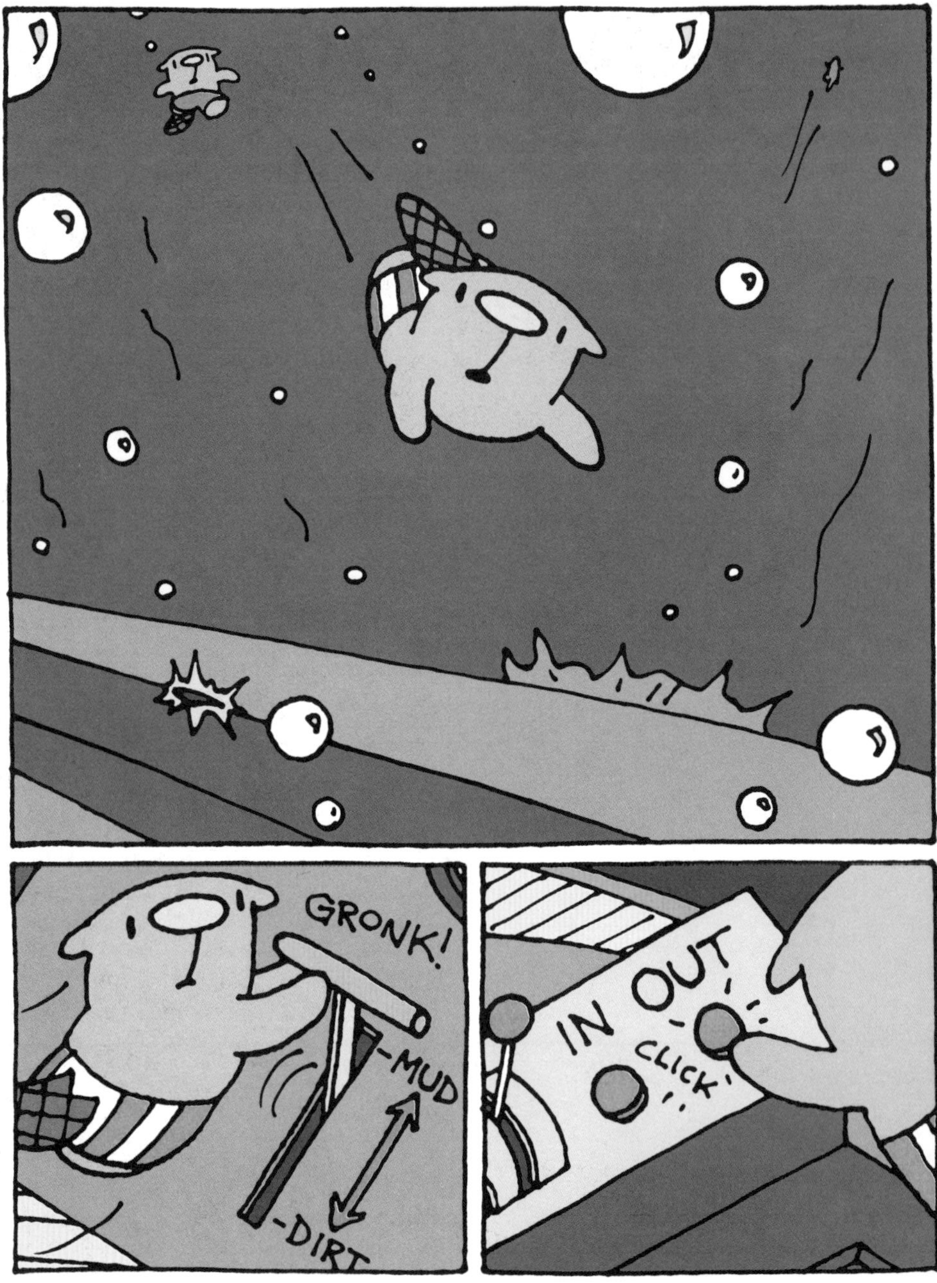
GRONK!
-MUD
-DIRT
IN OUT
CLICK

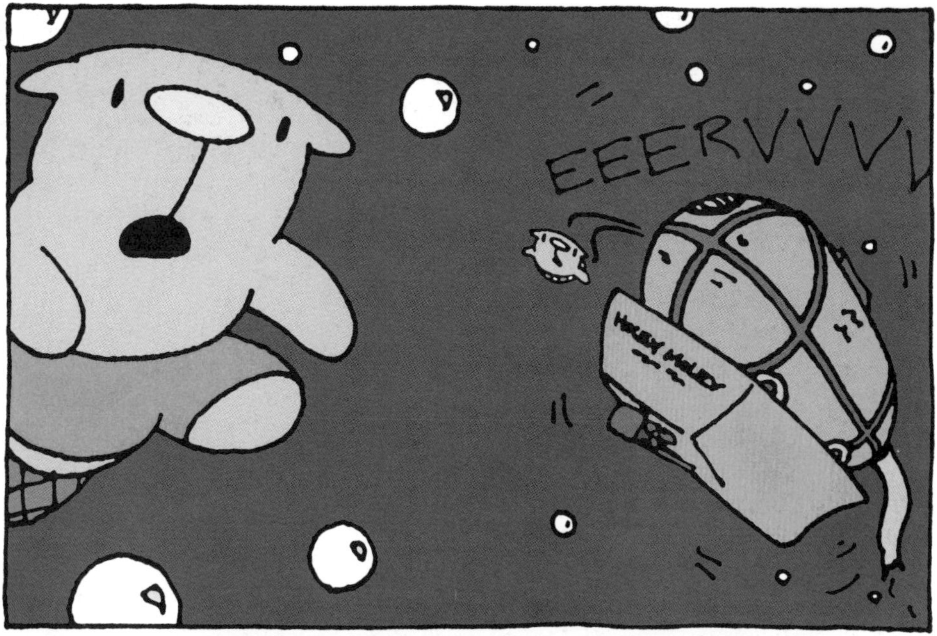
EEERVVVV

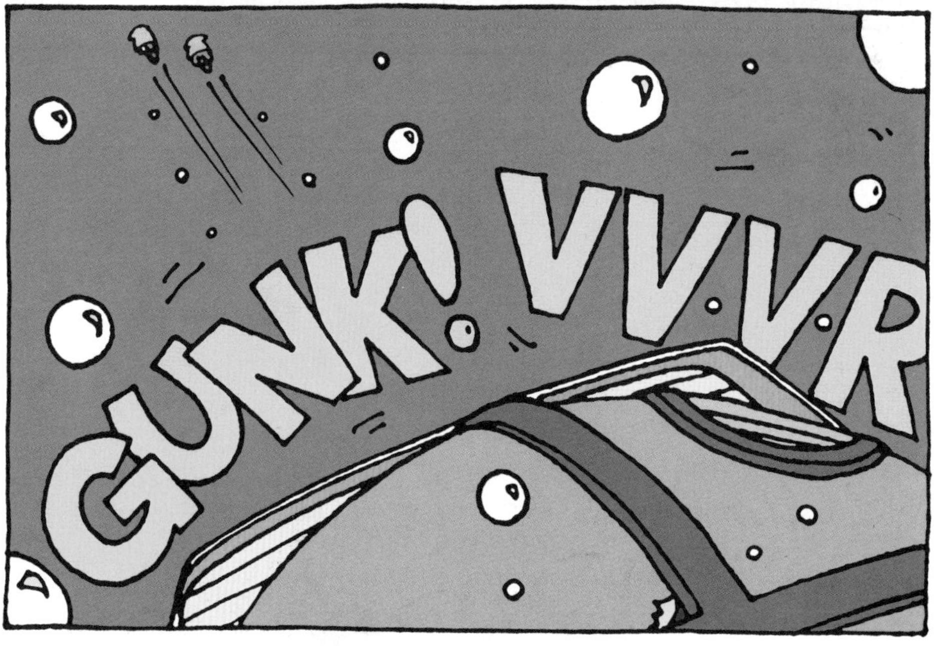
GUNK! VVVR

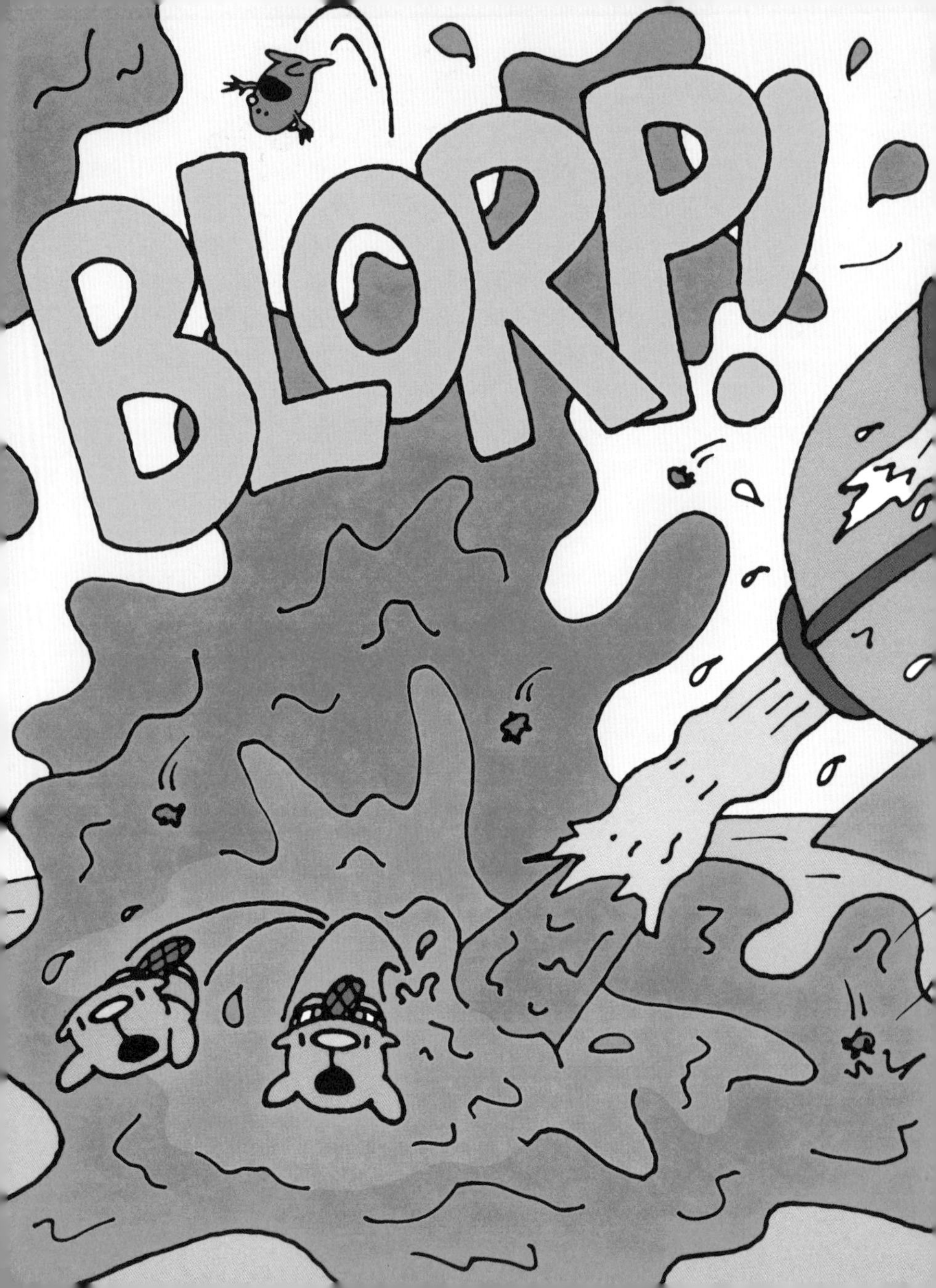
BLORP!

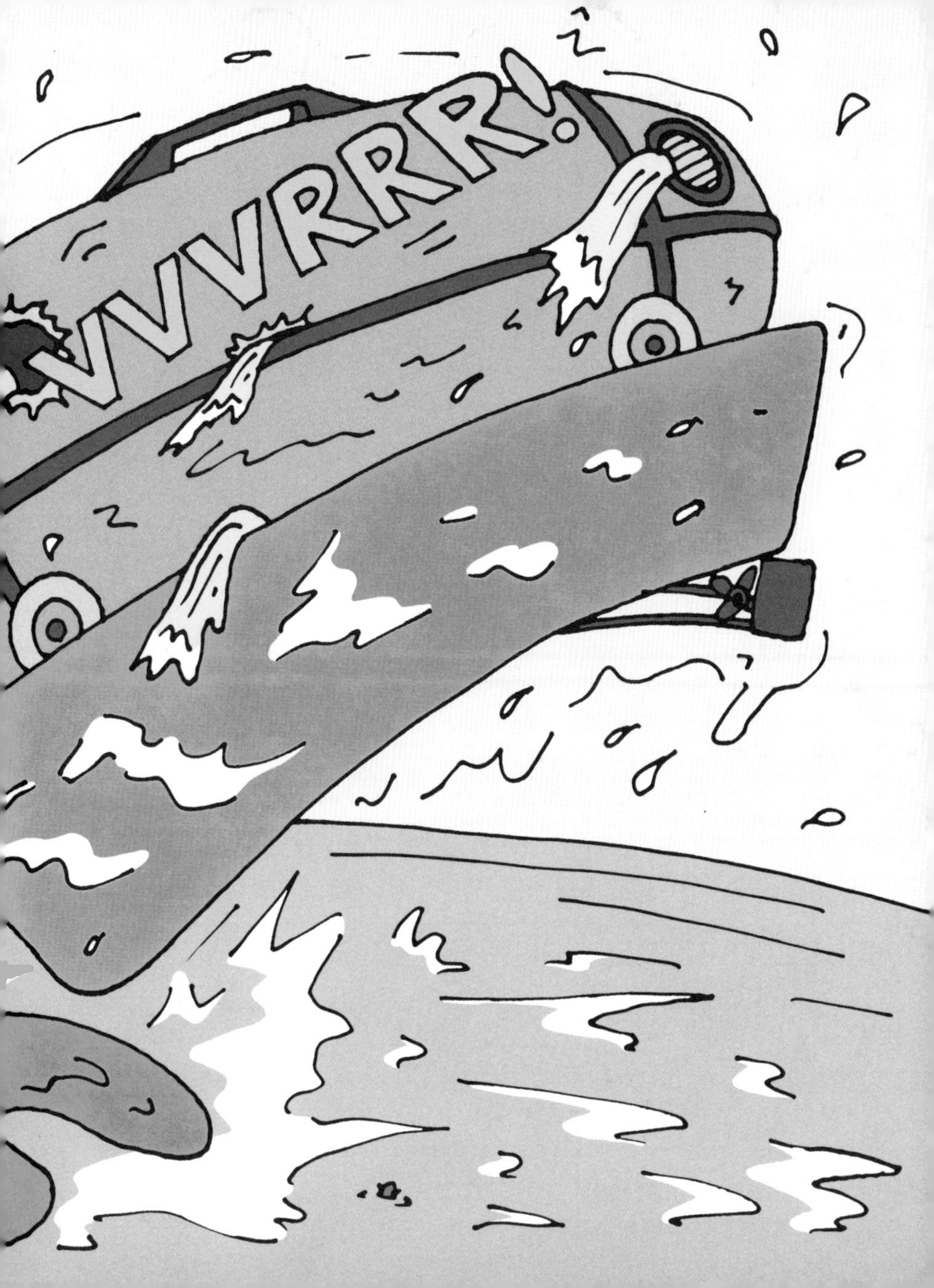
VVVRRR!

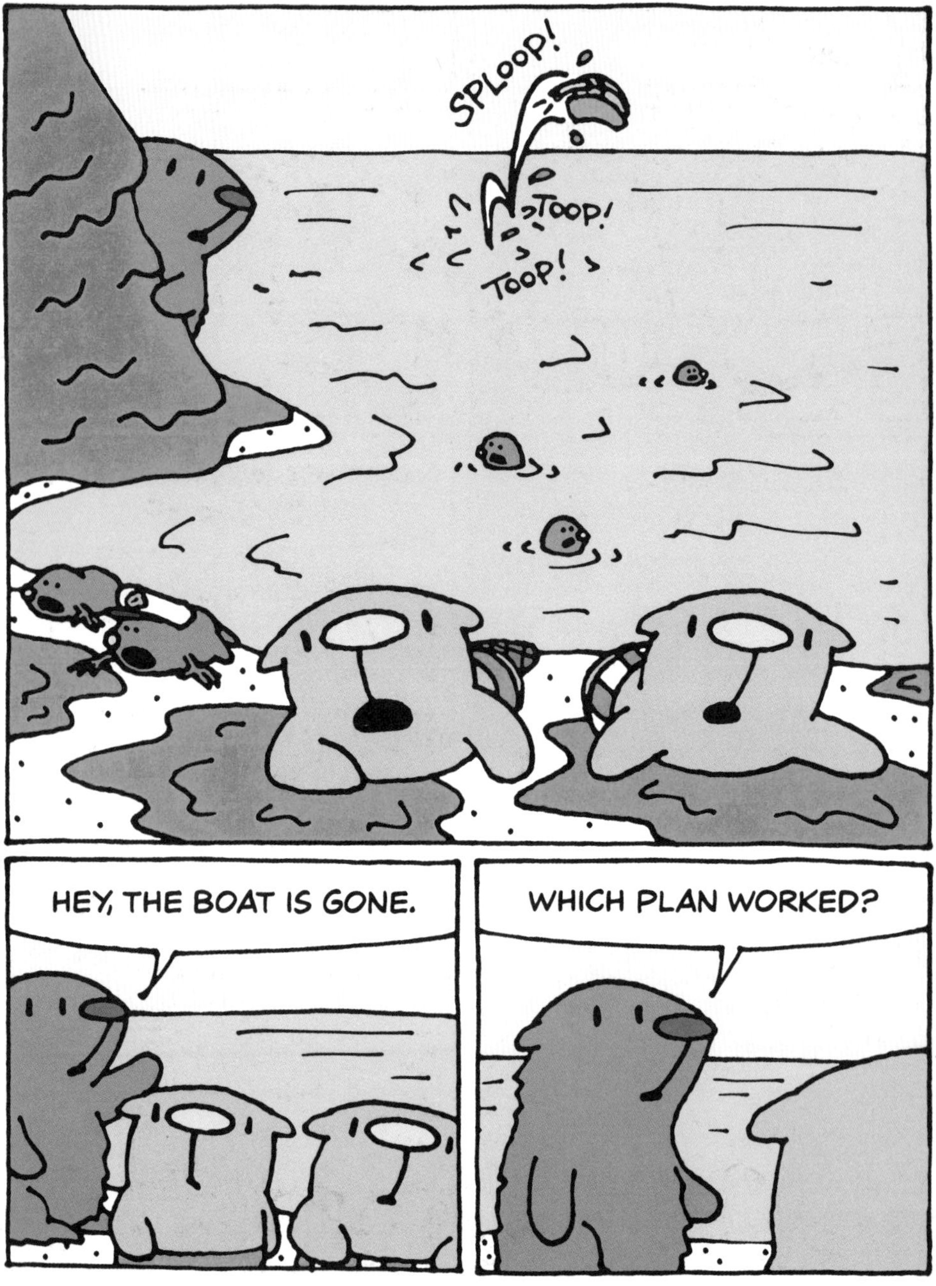
SPLOOP!
TOOP!
TOOP!
HEY, THE BOAT IS GONE.
WHICH PLAN WORKED?

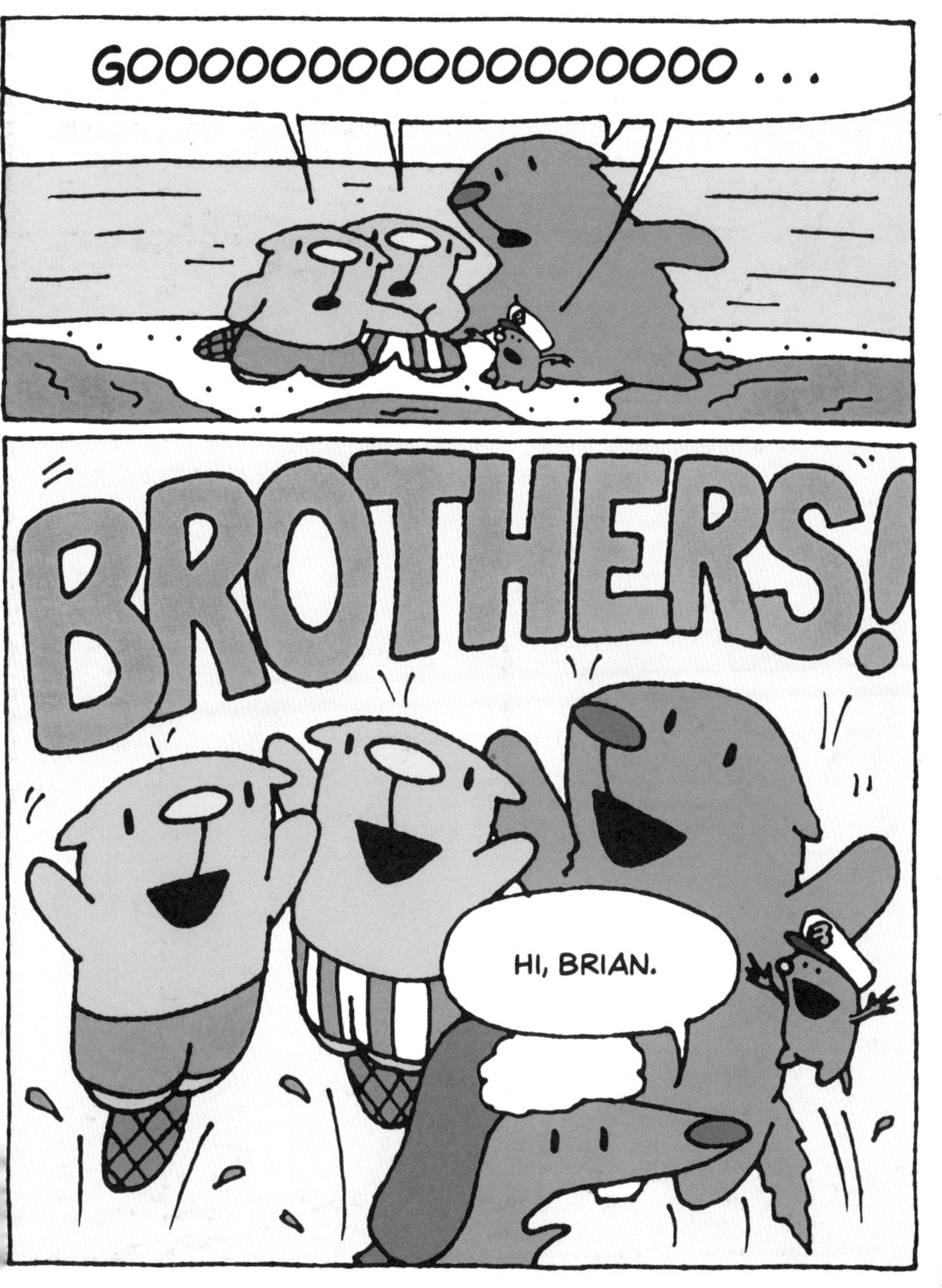
GOOOOOOOOOOOOOOOOOOO . . .
BROTHERS!
HI, BRIAN.